UNITED TATES of AMERICA

a novel with scrapbook art by
Paula Danziger

AN
APPLE
PAPERBACK

SCHOLASTIC INC.

New York   Toronto   London   Auckland   Sydney
Mexico City   New Delhi   Hong Kong   Buenos Aires

★ ★ ★ ★ ★ ★ ★ ★ ★ ★ ★ ★ ★ ★ ★ ★ ★ ★ ★

ISBN 0-590-69222-4

12 11 10 9 8 7 6   3 4 5 6 7/0

Printed in the U.S.A   40

First Scholastic paperback printing, November 2002

Book design by Steve Scott
The text type was set in Cooper Light.

★ ★ ★ ★ ★ ★ ★ ★ ★ ★ ★ ★ ★ ★ ★ ★ ★ ★ ★

Dedication

To the Raabs: Susan, David, Brian, Jeffrey, and Joshua
To Hannah Schwartz
To Heather Hebert

Chapter 1

My name is Skate Tate. I'm eleven years old and I've just about finished my first day of sixth grade at Biddle Middle. Actually, my first day has just about finished me. Skate Tate at Biddle Middle. It sounds like a Dr. Seuss book but it's not. . . . It's my life.

I'm the kind of kid who likes things that she likes to stay the same . . . and now a lot of things are different.

I have a whole new set of teachers. None of them know me, so they all call me Sarah Kate, my legal name. I have to convince them to call me by my nickname, Skate.

I don't think that it should be such a big deal for teachers to call me Skate. They really never knew me as Sarah Kate. It shouldn't be that hard to remember my name, even if it's not the one that is on their class list. After all, they have to call the school by a new name, too. It used to be called Clearglenn Regional Middle School. Now it's named for a principal, Clarence Biddle, who retired last June after twenty-seven and a half years. The rumor is that they promised to name it after him to get him to leave. Once, he lost an entire package of standardized tests. He left them at the Dairy Queen and the tests came back covered in chocolate-vanilla swirl with sprinkles all over them. So they convinced him to retire and now the school is named Biddle Middle.

Biddle Middle is so much bigger than Sendak Elementary. Five different towns send kids to this school, which is in Hammersmith, New Jersey. Hammersmith also has the local shopping mall. That would be very convenient if school officials scheduled shopping as one of the class electives . . . but they don't.

Back at Sendak Elementary, I had a routine and I liked it.

Every day, I would walk to school with my cousin, Susie. That took five minutes, forty-two seconds once we left her house, which is two minutes from mine. Running took three minutes and nineteen seconds. Hopscotching our way there took seven and three-quarter minutes. (We stopped doing that after third grade.) We'd go to the same classroom, with the same teacher. Then after school, we would go over to one of our houses and hang out, do homework together, and talk about just about everything. Then each of us would have dinner at our own house and then talk some more on the phone.

Now we have to ride the bus, which takes almost an hour each way. By car, it only takes about twenty minutes but, no, the bus stops every few minutes to pick up people. This morning, at the beginning of our first day, the ride was fun. We got to see a lot of kids from our town, Chelsea. Then there were four more towns and a gazillion more stops. A lot more kids got on. Some of them I knew from Soccer League, but a lot of them were strangers . . . and some of them were just very strange. . . . Three boys I never saw before got on and pretended that they were ducks. They duck danced their way up the aisle and sat way in the back, talking in some sort of duck language. A lot of the kids on the bus acted like it was a totally normal thing, the duck boys. Then, in the two rows in front of us, four eighth-grade boys decided to hold a farting contest . . . and there was no place for Susie and me to move. The bus driver stopped the bus four times to yell at everyone.

And today was just the beginning of a year of bus rides.

When we got to school, Susie and I had to go to different homerooms. We'd been in the same classes since second grade and now we have only one class and lunch together.

One good thing is that we're going to ride the bus home together and then go to my house, hang out, and talk about just about everything. Then Susie will go back to her house for dinner and then we'll call each other up and continue to talk.

The bell to end class is about to ring any second.

Mr. Booth, the science teacher, has given us an assignment and told us to start it immediately and silently.

Glancing up from my paper, I sneak a look at Mr. Booth, who has hair growing out of his ears. It was very hard to pay attention to what he was saying in class. I just kept staring at his ear hair, wondering if he ever trims it or if it will continue growing so that someday he'll be able to braid it.

I look down at my paper again.

I'll do my science homework tonight. I hope that Susie has the same homework and that we can do it together, but for now I want to make a list . . . of things that I can include in my scrapbook page of my first day of middle school.

1. English teacher — Mrs. Lipschitz — I like her a lot . . . her last name used to be Smith but she got married over the summer . . . lots of kids goof about her name but I'm not going to!

2. Social studies — Mr. Burke . . . he told us that his class is not the class where we can be social . . . I bet he says that every year.

3. Mrs. Einstein — math teacher. (I bet she married her husband just to have that last name.)

4. *Science* — *Mr. Booth is totally bald except for the hair growing out of his ears. [Paste real hair on his picture — I'll save some of mine when I get it cut . . . or maybe ask Susie for some since her hair is lighter than mine.]*

The bell rings.

I close my notebook, gather up all my belongings, and head to my locker.

I can't find it.

Back in elementary school, we had cubbies right in our class-rooms to store our things. Not only were there no locks on them, there were no doors.

Now we have hall lockers and I can't even figure out which hall my locker is in.

I rush.

If I miss my bus, I have to wait or take the late bus and then I won't be able to sit next to Susie.

I rush faster.

My locker is right where I left it.

I turn the combination lock.

It won't open.

I double check to make sure that it's my locker and then I double check to see if I got my combination right.

I try again.

I hit the door.

My hand hurts but it still won't open.

"Sixth grader." An eighth-grade boy, whose sister is on my soccer team, laughs as he walks past me without offering to help.

4

I hope that next year when he goes to high school, his locker won't open there and some senior makes fun of him.

I hope that this year . . . tomorrow in fact . . . the pimple on his nose pops open in lunch.

I hit the locker door again and this time it opens!

I rush out, hoping that Susie has gotten us good seats.

She's not there.

Chapter 2

No **Susie.**

I wonder what happened.

I hope that she's not lost at school.

I wonder if I should say something to the bus driver so that they can organize a search party.

Then I remember the time that our families went to Central Park Zoo when Susie and I were eight and Susie got lost. I was afraid that she had drowned in the seal pool or something . . . but she just went exploring on her own. We found her at the petting zoo.

I decide to wait, getting seats sort of near the front because all of the good seats in the back are already taken or being saved.

I put my backpack on the seat next to me.

Susie is still not there.

I keep telling people that the seat is taken.

I hope that she gets here soon.

Nina Carson gets on and says, "Hey, Skate. Susie said to tell you that she's got detention and she won't be on the bus. She'll call you tonight and tell you what happened."

I move my backpack so that Nina can sit down next to me, but she sits down next to Sal Flemington.

Susie's never gotten detention before. I wonder what she did.

It's a little weird.

It's only the first day. All new things are happening and the new things are changing already.

The three boys who act like ducks get on the bus and quack at everyone as they walk down the aisle.

Actually, they waddle down the aisle, quacking.

They're in my language arts class.

They were quiet in there.

Two of them sit down in the row across from me.

"Quack quack." The other one stands next to me. "That means . . . Move over. I want to sit down."

I debate telling him that he has to take the seat by the window, that I like the aisle seats and don't like being ordered around, but I decide not to.

Instead, I stare at him. "Say please."

He looks surprised, then nods and goes, "Quack."

I slide over.

Maybe next marking period I should sign up for a course called DSL, Duck as a Second Language.

I look out the window.

The boy next to me leans over and goes, "Quack, quack, quack," into my ear.

I ignore him.

He and his friends start quacking at one another.

I take out my notebook and continue the list that I started in study hall.

Duck Boy leans over and quacks at me again.

I look him in the eye and say, "Duck soup."

"Soup and quackers." He smiles.

I laugh.

He goes back to quacking with his friends, but for a moment I can see that there's a real person somewhere in there.

Then I go back to my notebook and continue writing down things that I will put in my scrapbook.

Notes:

5. I hope that we'll be able to play soccer in gym class. It's something that I'm very good at.

6. Shop. Not only is there no shopping there but I have to build a birdhouse in that stupid class. I really wanted art class . . . but NO. They gave me shop instead. I don't know why birds need houses when there are trees. Thirty people making thirty birdhouses . . . It'll be a housing development with feathers.

7. The library is really big . . . with a lot of books!!!!! That's so great. The school library in Chelsea is the size of a classroom, a very small classroom . . . and there are not a lot of books in it. Because of budget problems, there is no real Sendak Elementary librarian . . . just a retired computer teacher who comes in to work two days a week. He only bought computer stuff with the library money, which came to about thirty cents a student. Now we have a real librarian (who is also called The Media Specialist) and real books. I just hope that there is time to go to the library.

8. There are three boys in this school who act like ducks. Quacked!!!

The bus takes forever to get to Chelsea. The kids on our bus route who live closest to the school are so lucky. They get on last in the morning and get off first at the end of the day.

While I listen to everyone on the bus talk ... or quack ... I think about how I hope that Susie calls.

I can't wait to find out why she got detention.

Chapter 3

I'm home," I yell.

"We're in the kitchen," Mom calls out.

I put my books and backpack on the upstairs steps and then join them.

Mom and my little sister, Emma, are preparing our family's traditional "first day of school banquet."

Every year, on the first day of school, we serve Emma's and my favorite foods.

It's a family tradition.

Every year Mom, Emma, and I start preparation together, but now, for the first time, we couldn't because I was on the bus and I guess that waiting for me would have been silly and a waste of time.

I wish that they had waited anyway.

Our dog, Tunaburger, is sitting under the table, waiting for some food thing to drop.

The first year we made our first-day banquet, the meal was peanut butter and jelly sandwiches and spaghetti. (That was the year I *lived* on peanut butter and jelly.)

This year, it's going to be sushi (GUM, our wonderful Great-Uncle Mort, has taught me to eat things from all over the world, including uncooked fish!) and spaghetti. (Every year since pre-school, Emma has chosen spaghetti every time. She's in fourth grade now.)

"Did Susie call?" I ask, although I doubt she phoned from school.

My mom shakes her head no and then says, "Wasn't Susie on the bus with you?"

"She had to stay after school," I say and then change the subject because I don't want my cousin to get into trouble.

Our mothers are sisters and they tell each other practically everything.

"Let's get started on the sushi," I say, moving to the refrigerator.

Then, I look at my sister.

I look again.

She grins at me and then she notices that I am staring at her, a not-happy stare.

She's busted . . . caught wearing my new T-shirt, one that GUM sent, one that I've been saving for school.

Now that I leave earlier than she does, Emma has more of a chance to take my clothes.

I can see what she had for lunch from what is on MY T-shirt.

It was hot dog and bean day at Sendak Elementary.

"I was saving that for tomorrow," I say. "I love the photograph on it, the one by Ansel Adams."

Emma continues to bite on her lip.

I hope that she chews it off.

"Skate, don't be mad." She opens her blue eyes wide. "When I become a famous movie star, you can borrow my most amazing dress . . . the one that I will be wearing when I win the Oscar . . . or the one that I will be wearing when I win the Emmy and say, 'I would like to thank my beloved and very talented artist sister who throughout the years has shared with me not only her wisdom, but her T-shirts.'"

"Emma," I say.

She puts down the make-believe trophy and looks right into my eyes. "I'm sorry, Skate. Really truly. Don't be upset with me. If you are, my whole life will be ruined . . . ruined . . . ruined."

My sister looks down at the floor. "I'm really really sorry. Look, it's your turn to do the dishes tonight. I'll do them for you."

I think about it.

I hate doing dishes.

I also hate to give in so easily.

There's one tear coming down Emma's cheek.

She spent the summer practicing crying so that she will be ready in case she ever has to do a sad scene.

"I'm sorry," Emma repeats.

I make a decision.

"Okay," I say. "You can do the dishes and as long as the shirt cleans up, I won't be too mad at you."

"Thanks." She sighs a sigh of relief. "I just want you to know that it isn't my fault that the shirt got dirty. Some of the boys were screaming 'hot-dog poop' and throwing the beans."

Yuk . . . I remember those days at Sendak Elementary. The school is named after Maurice Sendak, the author and illustrator of *Where the Wild Things Are* . . . and it's true . . . Sendak Elementary sometimes is where the wild things are.

Emma takes off the shirt right here and hands it to our mother.

I remember when my chest was that flat . . . last year.

She goes upstairs to get another top.

"Skate," Mom says. "Let's prepare the sushi. You know Emma won't touch it. As she says, 'Slimy, yeechy, yuk.'"

I roll the rice into little balls, flatten it a little, and then put the raw fish piece on top of it, just the way GUM taught me to do.

Then I take a piece of dried seaweed, put rice and avocado and tuna in it, roll it up . . . and then cut it into slices.

Tunaburger keeps nudging at my knee, hoping that I'll feed her.

I don't.

Until Tunaburger eats sushi with chopsticks, she's not getting any.

Emma returns.

She's wearing an old T-shirt, one that I gave her when I outgrew it. I don't care how she garbages that one up.

She prepares her meal, putting water on to boil. Then she'll throw in the spaghetti and when it's all drained, she'll pour cold spaghetti sauce on it.

Mom will warm the sauce for the rest of us.

Emma grates the cheese.

She loves tons of cheese on top of the spaghetti.

Then we make the salad.

Every first day, Mom says that salad is her favorite food but I know it's not. She's just making sure that we eat healthy.

While we chop and peel, Emma and I take turns telling about the first day of school.

I tell them about the duck boys and show them the duck walk.

I tell Mom and Emma about how different things are in middle school, how much more grown up and mature it is than elementary school . . . and then I smile maturely at Emma.

Emma tells us that her teacher is Ms. Adams and then she makes a face. "I know that she is supposed to be good, but I wanted Mr. Jones."

"Because he is sooooooooooooo cute?" I ask.

She shakes her blond hair. "No. Ms. Adams expects me to be just like you. She asked if I was an artist. . . . I told her that I was just an okay artist but that I love acting. . . . I hate having the same teachers as you had. They always expect me to be just like you."

I look at my sister and think about how different we are in some ways.

She looks more like our cousin, Susie, than like me.

When we all go out together, everyone thinks that *they* are sisters.

She's blond and little.

13

I'm brown-haired and taller.

I love art and sports but hate to get up in front of people and give reports.

Emma likes sports but LOVES performing.

I'm glad that I'm the older sister, because if teachers thought I was going to be like her, I wouldn't like it any better than she does.

Soon the table is set.

Dad comes in.

He doesn't look happy.

I wonder if that's because he hates sushi as much as Emma does and knows that's on tonight's menu.

"Is everything okay?" my mom asks.

"I'm fine." He nods. "However, your car is not. The mechanic says that it's not worth sinking another penny into fixing it."

Mom's car. I love that car. My parents have pictures of us leaving the hospital in that car. . . . Brand-new baby. Brand-new used car.

It even has a name, Prunella.

And now Prunella is going to be gone.

My parents look at each other.

Dad just replaced his car last year, and I know that they're still paying it off.

Prunella is really good even though it is so old. It doesn't have to do much since Mom works at home and she only uses it for local things.

Mom sighs. "We'll just have to find one that's not too expensive. Until then you can use GUM's car. He said that we could use it anytime and it's just sitting there in the garage until he shows up again."

Great-Uncle Mort . . . GUM . . . I love his car. . . . It's an antique convertible. . . . When GUM is here, he and Dad work on it a lot.

My dad smiles, finally. He loves that car, too. "I don't feel totally right using it while he's away, but since this is an emergency, I guess I'm just going to have to drive Dr. Livingstone."

GUM's car is named after an explorer. When some reporter came to interview that explorer, he said, "Dr. Livingstone, I presume."

Now we all say that when we get into GUM's car.

It's a little dorky but it's a Tate family tradition.

Another Tate family tradition is naming our cars.

Dad's car is called Chargey . . . which is short for charged Charger, not named because the car was fast but because of the loan my parents took out to buy it.

I wonder what Mom's new car will be named.

I just hope that the car doesn't cost so much that we can't go on the big trip that we've been saving up for.

That's what happened when Dad got Chargey.

I wish that my family had a lot of money and didn't have to worry about anything.

Maybe if I wish hard enough, my wish will come true.

Chapter 4

ust as I get ready to do the assignment for Mrs. Lipschitz's class, the phone rings.

It's Susie.

It's about time.

I was getting really worried.

It turns out that Susie got detention for talking to someone named Kiki in math class.

Actually they both got detention.

Then afterward, Aunt Polly picked them up and took them out for dinner at Retroburger.

Susie sounds so happy, so excited. "Skate. Kiki is the best. She's interested in a lot of the things that I am. She's got great style . . . and knows so many kids."

I guess at this point I should say, "How wonderful!" but I don't.

Susie and I never even knew Kiki existed before today.

I think that Aunt Polly shouldn't have taken them both out for dinner after they had been punished.

I think that Susie should have called and asked me if I wanted to go.

I think that Kiki is a silly name. It sounds like a choking sound, Kiki.

Susie says, "Kiki is great. She's going to try out for the drama group and so am I."

I think about how Susie and I always used to work backstage on the Sendak plays.

Susie continues, "You know, Skate, back at Sendak, there were always the same people to know. . . . Well, now, there are so many more."

I want to ask her what's wrong with knowing the people you've always known and letting it go at that . . . but I don't say that.

Instead, I say, "So are you going to ride the bus with me anymore? Is Kiki on our bus?"

Susie giggles. "Of course I'm going to ride the bus with you . . . and no, boo hoo, Kiki is on another bus."

Then she tells me about her day and I start to tell her about mine.

Just as I relax, Susie says, "Call Waiting. Gotta check it out," and she switches to the other call.

When she comes on, she says, "Gotta take it. It's Kiki. We have to make some plans. See you tomorrow."

Susie hangs up.

I look at the phone in my hand.

There ought to be rules for Call Waiting.

If a person is already on the phone with someone and Call Waiting clicks in, the person can talk to the new caller but the person should not practically hang up on the first person who was on the phone . . . first. It makes the first person, ME, feel lousy . . . like someone else is more important.

The second rule is that the only exceptions are police emergencies, fires, parents, and people calling to say that you've won the lottery . . . or people calling to say that they are really choking to death.

I feel sad for a few minutes, thinking about the good old days . . . yesterday, when I was not only Susie's cousin, but also her best friend . . . thinking about Sendak Elementary, where I knew everyone, where everyone knew me, where I knew what to expect, and where we didn't even have lockers.

Then I look at my assignment book. Everything is done except for Mrs. Lipschitz's homework. I saved the best for last: language arts. I was all prepared for the traditional "What I Did Over the Summer Vacation" essay. I was going to tell her about day camp, about the riverboat trip we took with GUM, and about how I learned some new techniques to use in my scrapbooking . . . but no . . . for the first time in my first day of school writing history, I didn't get that assignment. (A good thing about Biddle Middle!) I have to write "Ten Things I Would Like Mrs. Lipschitz to Know About Me."

So here goes:

Ten Things About Skate Tate

1. *I like being called Skate Tate. I know that you have to use my "real" name, Sarah Kate, in the marking book, but please call me Skate and please let me use that name on my papers. Please!*

2. *My favorite subjects are art, reading, and writing.*

3. *I do not feel like making a birdhouse. I would rather be learning more about art! Industrial arts sounds like factories are turning art out and selling it in art shows in local hotels.*

4. *I've lived in Chelsea, N.J., for my entire life, all eleven years, and I like it a lot. It's very comfy.*

5. *I love to scrapbook. Do you know anything about*

scrapbooking? It's much more than just putting photos in an album. It's telling about life, memories, past and present. It's using photos, stickers, memory things, and writing. Sometime, if you want, I can show you some of the pages. The latest ones are of the trip we took with GUM (GUM is short for Great-Uncle Mort. GUM is my dad's uncle. My parents starting calling him that just before I was born.) Back to scrapbooking . . . there is a group of us who get together and "crop" (that's what making the pages is called). . . . We've been doing scrapbooking since Girl Scouts in the third grade. (Except for my sister, Emma, who started in the first grade.)

6. I have a major collection of smiley face things. Some people think that this is really doofy, but I don't care. Once GUM said that I have a smile "that lights up the sky" and he gave me a smiley-face toy that giggles and says, "That's funny." Since then, I've gotten lots of smiley face things. . . . Sometime, I can show you my smiley face pages.

7. My family is good. Mom is always saying what a close family we are and we are! Most of the time I like them a lot. Sometimes I don't, though, but I think that's normal, right?! My sister, Emma, is in the fourth grade. (Yup. That's right. Emma Tate. I don't know what my parents were thinking when they named her.) She wants to be a MOVIE STAR someday . . . and she's practicing now!!!!!!!

My parents are lots of fun, MOST of the time . . . but not ALL of the time. Dad's a college teacher (American studies) and he likes to have fun. (He does talk a lot about facts. Yawn!) My mom is a little more serious sometimes. She's a freelance copy editor. She reads things that are going to be printed, like books and articles, and she finds out what's wrong . . . spelling, grammar, facts, and stuff like that. (She says that it "drives her nuts" that I use so many .... and !!!!!!!!!!!!!!!!!!!!!!!! She also says that she tremendously dislikes it when I say, "So fun!" (I hope you don't mind...........

I like using that punctuation a lot!!!!!!!!!!!!!!!!!!!!!!! (It's so fun!!!!!!!!!!!!!!!!!!!!!)

We also have a dog, Tunaburger. (Emma named her.) Tunaburger's like a member of the family only she slobbers and barks and the rest of us don't, not usually (just joking!).

That's my "at home" family, but I have other relatives, too, who are very important. GUM is one of my favorite people in the whole entire world. He travels all over, sends us things from everywhere, and sometimes even takes us with him. (In fact, he has a small apartment, which is attached to our house. That's his permanent address but he is hardly ever here. Since he also has an apartment in San Francisco, sometimes he is there. . . . Usually, though, he's traveling. He can do that because when he was young, he invented some computer thingy and now he doesn't have to work at regular jobs anymore. He walks into a room and it's like something so wonderful is going to happen, going to be said. I love him soooooooooooooooo much!!!!!!

When he is around, I feel much more adventurous, much surer of things.) My Aunt Polly and Cousin Susie are also very close . . . in two ways. They live on the same block as my "home" family and I do . . . in fact, Susie is in our class. Susan Seinfeld in your marking book . . . we've always been cousins and best friends. . . . I hope that stays the same. . . . Daisy O'Donnell and Liberty Davis are my other best friends. They're almost like family. We've all known each other since Gymboree when we were four.

8. When I grow up, I want to be an artist. I'm not sure what kind, I just know that I want to be one, that I HAVE to be one.

9. I'm a doodler, Mrs. Lipschitz. Don't take it personally if I'm doodling in your class while you're speaking. I AM PAYING ATTENTION. Honest . . . I am. I just listen better when I doodle. Mr. Coburn, my fifth-grade teacher, didn't understand this, so last year I spent most of after-school life in detention. So, please, oh please, let me doodle while you

are speaking . . . and I will be one of your best students ever. And when I write something for class, please let me illustrate it, too!!!!!!

10. I hope that sixth grade turns out to be one of the best years of my life . . . NOT one of the worst ones.

Chapter 5

Today is the last day of the first week of school. Since we started on Wednesday, that means three days of school this week. I like that.

Actually, I have a great idea for how school should work . . . a four-day week . . . Mondays and Tuesdays in school . . . Wednesdays off, a mini-vacation . . . and then back for Thursdays and Fridays . . . and then it's the weekend.

Sitting in Mrs. Lipschitz's class, I'm waiting for class to start and looking at my cousin, Susie.

Susie has started dressing like Kiki. She's saying things like "Wowsey." And "Getta look at that." And "I'll be a marsupial's aunt." Which are all things that Kiki and her friends say.

It's like a science fiction movie.

My cousin has been taken over by the sixth-grade podgirls.

She still sits next to me on the bus and she says that she's planning to come to the scrapbooking crop this weekend, but she is sooooo different.

I don't understand how someone can change so quickly.

I always thought Susie liked the way she was.

I liked the way she was.

"Okay, class, now settle down." Mrs. Lipschitz pulls out her attendance book.

Since she is still trying to learn each of our names, she looks at the seating chart and starts calling out names.

Some of the kids say, "Here."

Some say, "Present."

Joe Duey says, "Yo."

So do Hugh Fields and Lou Gregson.

These are the duck boys. At least they're not quacking.

"Hugh. Mr. Duey. Lou. Your fame precedes you," Mrs. Lipschitz says. "I have learned that because of your names you are called D.D.T., the Donald Duck Trio . . . Huey, Duey, and Louie."

The three of them quack.

"Very comic." Mrs. Lipschitz stares at them and makes the stern teacher face at them.

They quack again.

"That's it," she says. "No more fowl behavior."

Some of us laugh.

Mrs. Lipschitz even smiles, but then she says, "I want this class to know that while I believe in having fun, there's a time and a place for everything. There are certain things that I will not tolerate."

We all get very quiet.

She looks back down at the seating chart and says, "I'm going to do a little rearranging."

The three boys are moved to the front.

That means that three of us are moved to the back . . . Scott Sherman, Julianna Barton, and me.

It's very annoying when you haven't done anything wrong and get moved anyway.

It's also not so annoying because I get to sit in the back and doodle without being so noticed.

I wonder if Mrs. Lipschitz moved me because of that or if I was just moved.

It's not always easy to figure out how teachers' brains work, especially not at the beginning of the year.

Mrs. Lipschitz walks around the room, returning papers, the assignments about the ten things we want her to know about us.

"Class," she says, grinning. "I want you to appreciate the fact that I have written a response to each and every one of your essays. That's thirty responses to this class and thirty-two to my other language arts–English class."

Someone claps.

Soon everyone is clapping.

She takes a bow. "Thank you. Thank you. Thank you. Don't expect that for every assignment, especially once work on the newspaper starts. I'm the adviser and would like to invite all of you to come to the meeting on Monday after school."

The school newspaper sounds like fun.

I look down at my paper.

She's written a lot.

I remember last year . . . how Mr. Coburn hardly ever corrected our papers. He said that he threw them up in the air and whichever ones ended up on top got A's. . . . The ones on the bottom got F's. Last year, I used very lightweight paper just in case that was true. I'm not sure, though. At the end of the marking period, we just got grades on our report cards and most of us never understood why. We'd complain. He'd shrug.

I look down at what she's written:

Dear Skate,

I really liked your list and look forward to learning a lot more about you.

I am not positive about how I feel about your doodling. So here is my decision, for the time being. While taking notes, you may doodle. However, you may not doodle on test papers or on most homework assignments, unless preapproved. As the year progresses, we will evaluate whether this system works. Just know that I DO NOT like messy papers. Since you are so interested in art, why don't you come to the meeting of <u>The Biddle Bulletin</u>? We're looking for a cartoonist, and I think you should try out.

I am not enamored of the overuse of exclamation marks and dots. I do not think it is "so fun!" I don't even think it's "so much fun."

Thanks for telling me about your family. It must be wonderful to have an uncle who is so adventurous. When he returns to Chelsea, it would be terrific if he could come into our class and talk about some of the exciting places he has visited. (This year I am going to try to bring in a lot of different speakers.)

Skate, guess what? I am a scrapbooker, too. In fact, when I was doing lesson plans this summer, I decided to have the class do some scrapbooking in conjunction with our lessons. It's terrific knowing that some of you already scrap.

Let's all work together to make this class a great experience.

Sincerely,

Mrs. Lipschitz

Third day in class and already I have a lot to look forward to.
I'm going to *The Biddle Bulletin* meeting on Monday after school.
Skate Tate, cartoonist.
I really do want to be an artist.
I really want to be chosen.
I wonder if I will be chosen?
I'm going to do the best I can.
I really want to be chosen.
. . . And I can't wait until the next time GUM calls and I can ask
him when he's going to be back and please please please come to
our class.

Chapter 6

It's Friday . . . the end of my first week.

Getting off the bus, I think about how tomorrow will be the first fall meeting of The Happy Scrappys.

Everyone is coming to the meeting.

Susie said at first that she wasn't sure she could make it but then she said that she could.

I think that she was hoping to do something with Kiki but I think that Ms. Kiki has some sort of lesson tomorrow . . . drama or dance or wonderfulness, or something.

I thought that Susie would come over after school today but she's staying after school with Kiki, who's trying out for drama club.

I'm glad that Susie will be at The Happy Scrappys tomorrow.

It's so different not seeing her all the time.

I'm afraid that I'm not so important to Susie anymore.

Opening the front door to my house, I call out, "Mom. I'm home."

She calls back, "In the kitchen. Hurry up. I have a surprise for you."

I rush into the kitchen, wondering what the surprise is.

Maybe she's made my favorite dessert, chocolate cheesecake.

I enter the kitchen.

It's not chocolate cheesecake.

It's even better.

In the chair, across from my mom, is one of my favorite people in the whole entire world.

I say what I always say when I see him sitting down, "Watch out, there's GUM on the chair."

"Okay kiddo. Skate on over here." He says what he always says when he first sees me. "Give your old Great-Uncle Mort a big hug."

Then I rush over to him.

I say, "You're not *so* old. If you were, we'd have to call you O'GUM . . . and we don't."

I look at GUM.

He's fifty-seven years old . . . that's not old-old . . . not ancient old. He was twenty years old when my dad, his nephew, was born.

I hug him and ask at the same time, "When did you get here? How long are you staying? Where are you going next? Do you think you can stay here for a while?"

He laughs. "Slow down . . . enough questions for a minute . . . and you forgot an important one . . . one that you always asked first, when you were little."

I grin at him.

"Ask." He grins back.

I know which question he is talking about but now that I am older, I don't ask this anymore even though I do think it.

"Ask," he says. "It's okay."

I look at my mother, who taught us not to ask.

She grins, shrugs, and says, "With GUM, the rules are different. You can ask."

"What did you bring me? What did you bring me?" I clap my hands and jump up and down. "What did you bring me?"

Once I start asking, it's hard to stop.

GUM goes over to a suitcase, opens it up, and pulls out a large package with my name on it. "Gifts from India."

The package is filled with lots of smaller packages.

I open one.

Paper . . . it's absolutely amazing. It looks like there are things in it. I touch it, smile, and think about how I'm going to use it in my artwork.

"It's all handmade," GUM tells me. "I visited the factory. They add things like flowers, onion skin, garlic, and fabric."

I open a bag filled with squares of fabric . . . silks and suedes and beautiful patterns. "Oh, GUM . . . this is wonderful! I love it. Thank you."

"I thought you could use it in your scrapbooks," GUM says.

I smile at him. I'm smiling so much that it feels like my face is going to break.

GUM is always interested in my artwork.

I remember when I was in second grade and making Popsicle stick log cabins.

GUM and I must have eaten a gazillion pops until we realized that craft stores sold the sticks without the ices.

My Popsicle stick village was very colorful.

I open another package.

"Oh, GUM . . . these are beautiful. What are they?"

"They're called *bindis*." He explains, "Indian women wear them on their foreheads."

Bindis . . . tiny little dots and other shapes . . . all different kinds . . . material, jewels, plastic, a mixture of all three . . . I just love them.

I open another package . . . bracelets . . . large and small.

I hold up one of the tiny ones. "Too large for a ring . . . too small for a bracelet."

GUM and I look at each other and say at the same time, "Picture frames."

I pass them over to my mom to look at and she says, "GUM gave some to me, too. I'm going to use them as napkin rings."

Another package to open . . . and it's beautiful material.

GUM says, "It's an Indian sari, a dress."

"Who's sari now?" My mom sings an old song that she likes, "Who's Sorry Now."

GUM and I groan and cover our ears.

GUM grins at me. "The D.F. not only has the family habit of punning . . . she has the family habit of not being able to sing on key."

GUM calls Mom The D.F., the Delicate Flower, because she doesn't like to rough it, to camp out when we travel.

I open the last package.

Art books from India . . . the work is so beautiful.

I just keep smiling at GUM, who keeps smiling back.

I am so happy.

Even if GUM had arrived with no gifts, I would still be so happy. Being with GUM is the best gift of all.

I remember something.

"GUM," I say, using the voice that says, "Please oh please" without having to say, "Please oh please."

"Yes," he says, making "yes" take several seconds to come out of his mouth.

That "yes" means "Yes . . . what do you want?" . . . and "Yes . . . I'll probably do it."

We grin at each other.

GUM and I are members of the mutual grinning society.

"I wrote about you and now my teacher wants you to come to class to tell everyone about your adventures," I inform him.

He makes a face and says, "Now, let me think about that."

I know GUM. He'll act like he's thinking about it but then he'll say, "Yes."

My mom and I look at each other while he keeps saying, "Hmmm. Let me think about this."

I cross my eyes.

She crosses her eyes and then looks at her watch.

He goes "Hmmm" a few more times.

My mom looks at her watch again and says, "Come on, Mort . . . time's a-wasting."

He grins at her and then looks at me and says, "Oh, okay."

I go over and kiss him on his head.

"But," he says, "before I go to your school, I have some business in New York. I won't be around for a couple of days, so let's plan on my going in the middle of next week."

"Hooray!" I clap my hands.

I can't wait for Mrs. Lipschitz and my class to meet him and hear about all the amazing places he's gone.

It's so wonderful that he's my GUM.

I just know that they are going to love him as much as I do.

Chapter 7

It's **Saturday** and The Happy Scrappys are getting together at my house for the first time in the new school year.

All five of us are here . . . Emma, Daisy, Liberty, Susie, and I.

I'm so glad that we are meeting. Things are changing a lot and this is one thing that I want to stay the same.

We haven't gotten together as The Happy Scrappys since the end of last school year.

At the first meeting, we have a tradition. Each of us does a personal page to put in *The Happy Scrappys* yearbook. Then we work on our own scrapbooks.

Every year, someone does the cover and this year it's my turn.

I've scanned and reduced each of our individual pages — put them on the cover — and added all sorts of stickers to it.

Once the pages and cover are done, we put it all together. I scan each page, make five copies, and ta-da . . . we have a yearbook to remind of us what we were like at different points of our lives. Since we've been doing this since third grade, the books are a little like histories. Sometimes they are embarrassing histories. I can't believe how I dressed in the fourth grade.

We've got photos, postcards, and things that we've collected that will go into our own memory albums. We've also got the things that we've bought over the years in stores . . . paper, stickers (big and little, long ones used as borders), rubber stamps, page headings, special scissors, glue, sticky dots, circle cutters, photo corners . . . so much stuff . . . so much allowance.

I've even got a great machine that GUM gave me for Christmas last year. It laminates and it turns things into stickers.

"Trade time," Emma calls out. "Anyone got a soccer T-shirt die-cut?"

I look through my collection of paper which is cut into different shapes and shake my head.

"I've got four," Liberty offers. "All different sizes."

"I've got a tie-dye die-cut one." Susie holds up a piece of paper.

I walk around and look at all of the scrapbooking material choices.

Daisy looks at all of my supplies and we negotiate a trade. She really likes my large dog sticker, since she has a large dog.

Susie is very excited to see my collection of "jewels" that she wants to use on her page.

I happily trade with her, taking some of her design line stickers.

She seems quite happy.

So am I.

The two tables are set up and we're all working on our pages.

"Oh, Skate, do you have an extra critter sticker?" Susie asks.

I show her the sticker sheet, she makes her choice, and then I pick out a smiley face sticker that I don't already have.

Soon, we're all making trades.

"I'm tired of my star punch." Liberty holds it up.

"Oooooh, my life would be complete with one," Emma says.

My sister really is Queen of Drama.

They trade.

Apparently Liberty's life will be complete with a unicorn rubber stamp.

Then it's back to work on our pages.

I look over at Emma, who has somehow gotten a sticker on her nose.

"Emma," I say, "nose. Duh."

She takes off the sticker and then sticks her tongue out at me for no reason at all.

I stick my tongue out at Emma.

She pretends to pick her nose and flick it at me.

I make a face at her. "Oh, that's really attractive. Someday, if you become famous and *People* magazine does an article about you, I'll be sure to mention that you do that. Then millions will know how disgusting you are."

"*People* magazine." She grins. "I'm ready."

"For what? To be in their list of hundred most nose-picking people?" I make a face, trying to look totally disgusted.

"Aaaaaarg," Daisy says, "I just nicked myself and now a little bit of blood is on my page."

"Double aaaaaarg," I say, sorry that it has happened to her but glad that it hasn't happened to me. I hate when I work on a page for hours and then something happens that messes it up, especially when I've already glued and taped everything down.

I get up and look at it.

It doesn't look great, but it's a little dot of blood, not a huge glob of it.

Daisy says, "Oh well, I'll find a sticker or die-cut that will cover it."

While she looks through her stickers and the paper shapes, I go back to my page.

I like the way it's turning out.

When I'm old, like in my thirties and forties and then later when I'm really old, I'll be able to look back at the scrapbooks and re-member the good old days.

There's a picture of everyone: Skate Tate, Emma Tate, Susie Seinfeld, Daisy O'Donnell, Liberty Davis . . . The Happy Scrappys.

(That was a name that we came up with in the third grade. It's an okay name . . . except Huey, Duey, and Louie called us The Happys Crappys when they heard us talking at school about today's meeting. They can be such clucks! They also called Daisy "Aunt Daisy.")

"Snack time." Mom walks into the rec room, which by this time The Happy Scrappys have turned into the wreck room.

We all take a few minutes to finish whatever we're working on, clean up a little, and go into the kitchen.

Mom checks each one of us out to make sure that we aren't bringing in paint, glue, glitter, or stickers that can get over any furniture or anything. It's a little embarrassing. We're not in the third grade anymore.

She walks around, saying, "Sticker Patrol," pulling stickers off everyone and putting the stickers on a piece of waxed paper.

Mom pulls stickers off my legs. I don't know how they got there.

Stickers seem to have a way of escaping from the sheets of paper and attaching themselves to other things.

When she gets to Daisy, she double checks everything.

Mom takes eleven stickers, four die-cuts, and a Scotch tape roll off Daisy.

We all grab pieces of pizza and cans of soda and then sit down.

It's time to eat. It's time to talk, even though we keep doing that while we work.

And then it's time to get back to our scrapbooks.

Chapter 8

The **Biddle Bulletin** meeting is about to start.

I'm sitting in the back of the room.

Most of the sixth graders are in the back of the room with the eighth graders in the front.

When we went to Sendak Elementary and got to fifth grade, we were the big deals, the oldest kids in the school, the top of the heap.

Now we are the little deals, the youngest kids in the school, the bottom of the heap.

I'm having a good time, anyway, so far.

I look to the front and see that Heather Henderson is sitting up there, even though she is a sixth grader . . . because she's going out with an eighth grader, Eric Drew.

Eric is editor in chief.

Heather likes going out with guys who are in charge.

I think that this is one of her traditions.

It all started when Scott Sherman was chosen feeder of the goldfish in first grade. Heather thought that since he was in charge of the class pet, that made Scott teacher's pet. Heather went up to him and told him that he was now her boyfriend. He punched her in the nose but that hasn't stopped Heather from always wanting to be the girlfriend of the boy who is in charge. It drives her nuts when some girl is in charge. Sometimes I wish that she would just try to be the one in charge, but I don't think that's going to happen.

Heather wants her own gossip column.

I look around the room.

Garth Garrison is here.

Ever since second grade, he's drawn superhero comic strips and he's great.

I'm getting nervous.

I never thought that he would be here.

Garth never joins any club or group.

At least he never did.

I wish that he didn't decide to do it now.

I take a deep breath and try to calm down.

Trying out for the paper is making me nervous . . . but I really want the chance to do artwork.

Knowing that I will be competing against a really good artist like Garth makes me even more nervous.

GUM always says that a person isn't going to know what he or she can do unless that person tries to do it . . . and then if it doesn't work out, tries again.

I want to do the art.

I know that I can do the art.

I'm going to try.

If someone else gets chosen, I guess I'll live.

I bet Leonardo da Vinci and Michelangelo were never artists on their school newspaper . . . and they did all right.

I continue to look around.

Mindy Farley is here.

She wants to be an investigative reporter.

Mindy is chewing on her pencil eraser.

Mindy always chews on her pencil eraser.

I wonder what the inside of her stomach looks like, if half of it has been erased.

I don't even want to think about how it looks when the eraser pieces leave her body.

Huey, Duey, and Louie walk in.

Actually, they waddle in, quack, and sit down.

"Boys," Mrs. Lipschitz says. "This is a meeting of *The Biddle Bulletin,* not detention."

"We don't have detention today," Huey says. "We're here because we want to be sports reporters."

Marty Ross, who is the sports editor, puts his head down on the desk.

"We're serious," Louie says.

Huey and Duey quack.

Marty Ross bangs his head on his desk.

Huey grins. "We figure that we will be very good at it, especially covering football games."

"First down," Duey says. "Get it . . . ducks covering down."

Marty Ross looks at Mrs. Lipschitz and then pretends to die.

Mrs. Lipshitz looks at Marty and then at the D.D.T. Duey repeats, "First down." Huey says, "Second down." They both look at Louie, who says, "Sit down."

They look surprised but then laugh and sit.

Mrs. Lipschitz frowns and then sighs. "I'm trying to be patient with the three of you, but watch your step."

Then she announces to everyone, "For all of you who are seriously interested in becoming part of the newspaper staff, I wish that you could all get positions on the paper, but sadly, that can't happen. Those of you who don't make it may still have the opportunity to contribute to the newspaper. There will be chances to freelance."

While freelance sounds like a fencer who gets his or her weapon without paying for it, I know that it really means that a person can do work without belonging to a company. My mom is a freelancer. I also know that it isn't the same as working all the time in the same place. At least my mom can work for lots of different companies.

It's not as if I can work on lots of different middle school newspapers!

I don't want to be a freelancer. I want to be a regular.

Mrs. Lipschitz continues to talk about the responsibility of being on the paper.

There's not a quack out of Huey, Duey, or Louie.

I take out my notebook and start doodling.

Looking over, I can see that Garth is also doodling.

Mrs. Lipschitz hands out packets with assignments and applications.

Articles and columns to write . . . cartoons and illustrations to do . . . work to edit and proofread. . . . There's a lot more to putting together a newspaper than I thought.

There's no question of what I'm going to try out for. . . . The only question is what to draw so that I get chosen.

Mrs. Lipschitz continues to talk for a few more minutes, and then the eighth graders who are editors speak.

There is no art editor because Donny Haselfieffer and his family moved over the summer. So Mrs. Lipschitz explains that what is really needed is one artist, one who will be named art editor.

Garth Garrison and I look at each other.

Then we each look away.

The rest of the editors explain what is needed, what their staffs will do, the amount of time it will all take.

I think about the speech that I will make when I am art editor, if I am art editor.

I look again at Garth Garrison, who seems to be looking at me.

I wish that he wasn't such a good artist.

Finally, Mrs. Lipschitz looks at her watch and says, "Time's up. The late bus will be here in ten minutes. Eighth graders, tomorrow morning we'll use homeroom time and activity time to plan the first issue. . . . Oh, and those of you who are chosen will be changing homerooms and may have to make some changes in your schedules."

I will gladly change homerooms. I also will gladly not take industrial arts.

Leaving the room, I rush to my locker and then to the bus.

Huey, Duey, and Louie sit behind me.

They talk to one another, using a combination of pig latin and quacks. Someone told me that they've been talking like that since third grade.

"Iayquack opehayquack hattayquack ewayquack ecomebayquack portsayquack eportersrayquack," Louie says.

"Emayquack ootayquack," Huey says.

Duey just quacks.

After a few days of listening to them, I can figure out their duck language.

Louie hopes that they become sports reporters. Huey hopes for the same thing. Duey just ducks talking about the subject.

Pulling a notepad and pen out of my backpack, I start taking notes and making sketches.

I continue to sketch on the bus.

Susie's not there.

She and Kiki have detention again.

As soon as I get home, I can go up to my room and get to work immediately.

I really want to be on *The Biddle Bulletin*.

That way I will feel like I really belong at Biddle Middle.

Chapter 9

How come Skate gets to have GUM come to her class and not me?" Emma goes into one of her major pouts.

"Because I asked GUM to my class. I didn't ask you." I smile sweetly.

"I don't mean that." Emma stamps her foot. "I don't want to come to your stupid class. I want GUM to come to MY class."

"To your stupid class?" I continue to smile.

Emma escalates, combining a major pout with a full-fledged snit.

If this were an Olympic event, I would give her a 10.0 on the snit and a 9.9 on the pout. Her lip would have to be out just a little more to get a perfect score.

Emma stamps her foot. "Not funny . . . just because you are older, you get everything first . . . and now GUM is coming to your class first. It isn't fair."

She stamps her foot again.

She loses points for stamping her left foot with her right foot. 6.8.

However, her lip goes out, so that moves the pout score up to 10.0.

I just keep smiling.

It's not that I want to torment Emma, but if she's asking for it . . . then I don't mind doing it.

The front doorbell rings.

It's GUM.

Emma says, "How come you're going to Skate's class and not mine? Is it because you love her more than you love me?"

"Yes, it is," I say, because Emma is really getting on my nerves.

"No, Emma." GUM looks at her. "I love you both the same."

There are tears coming down Emma's face.

This time I think that they are real tears, not her fake ones, and I feel bad for her. "Look, Emma," I say. "I bet if GUM didn't have to go back to New York for some more appointments and then have to leave on Thursday to catch the plane to Bermuda, he would go to your class, too."

GUM nods. "Next time I'll come to your class."

"Promise." Emma wipes her eyes.

"Promise." He nods again.

"Cross your heart and hope to die." Emma crosses her heart and looks at him.

He looks a little surprised and then says, "Cross my heart. Emma, you can tell your class . . . next time I will speak to them."

"You didn't say 'and hope to die,'" Emma tells him. "You don't really mean it if you don't say that."

GUM says nothing.

"Oh, grow up." I shake my head. "Emma, stop being such a pain."

"If he doesn't say the whole thing, he doesn't mean it." She looks very serious.

GUM stands there and then he says, "Cross my heart and hope to die."

Emma rushes over and gives him a huge hug.

He hugs her back and then says the thing that he always says to her. "Accept no imitations . . . only accept Emma Tate tions."

Huggy huggy . . . I think and then say, "Emma, you'll be late if you don't leave soon."

Emma keeps stalling, but finally it's time for her to go.

GUM and Mom and I sit down and have a cup of coffee.

I get to go to school a little later because I am bringing in the guest.

I take a sip of coffee.

I don't really like coffee, but it makes me feel all grown up and special to be drinking coffee with them.

We look at some of the things that GUM is going to show.

"Objects and artifacts," he says. "I've brought my travel log so that your classmates can see all of the places that I've been . . . and I've brought some slides. But don't worry, I haven't brought a lot. I know how boring watching a lot of slides can be. I've only brought some of the spectacular ones and some of the funny ones."

That's one of the things I like about GUM. He cares about not boring kids.

"I've collected some of the things that you've sent us or brought back." Mom shows us what she has chosen.

There are postcards from all over the world . . . fabrics, a tiled elephant from the place in India where the Taj Mahal is, aboriginal bark paintings from Australia . . . tams from Scotland . . . amber from Poland . . . beautiful embroidered dresses from Hungary that Emma and I wore when we were very little . . . a pipe from Germany . . . small Inuit carvings from Alaska . . .

My mom looks at everything that is on the table. "I just brought a few things down. Is there anything else that you want to take?"

"My smile phone." I grin.

We all laugh.

GUM brought this big package all the way back from Singapore and then when we looked at where it came from, we found out it was Long Island.

The phone went all the way from Long Island, New York, to Singapore and back to the U.S., to New Jersey.

"I love it," I say. "And I've never seen one like it here in America."

"Anything for your smile collection." GUM says it like he means, "Anything for you, Skate Tate."

I look at GUM and think about how much I love him . . . and am glad that he loves me so much, too.

It makes me feel very special.

"It's time to go to school, Skate," my mom says. "You two have a great time."

GUM and I go out to the car.

First I say, "Dr. Livingstone, I presume," and then we get into the car.

On the way there, GUM asks, "So, honey, how do you like middle school?"

I tell him that I'm not sure, that I'm kind of watching and trying to figure things out.

I tell him that I miss the way things were in elementary school.

GUM stops at a red light and looks over at me. "Skate. Why don't you think of Biddle Middle as a trip, a journey."

"But on a trip, I get to go home again . . . to the way that things normally are." I bite my lip.

The light changes and the car moves forward.

GUM thinks for a few minutes and then he says, "Whenever I travel, I try to learn as much as I can about a place . . . and then I do the things that I like."

"It doesn't work that way in school, GUM," I remind him. "In school, we have to do things that we don't like . . . like build bird-houses."

He nods. "You're right. You know, Skate, sometimes on trips things don't always happen the way I want them to, BUT I try to think of it as an adventure, as a way to learn new things that become part of who I am."

46

"Did you feel that way when you were a kid? When you were my age?"

He smiles and then laughs. "No, actually I didn't . . . but I'm a lot wiser now and want you to learn things that will work for you, make life much fuller, much more comfortable."

I sigh.

He turns the car into the school driveway. "I guess there are just some things that you are going to have to learn on your own, some things that you are going to decide whether you want to do or not."

I sigh again, thinking about how hard it is to be a kid sometimes.

He smiles at me. "There's no right or wrong in this. Don't worry, honey. You'll figure it all out."

"And you can help me." I smile at him.

GUM parks the car in the principal's spot.

He's not really good about authority.

Dad says that's why it's good that GUM always worked for himself, creating computer games and programs that everyone wanted.

GUM not only got to be his own boss, he got to retire really early and travel the world.

I try to explain that the principal gets very cranky when someone takes his parking space.

GUM just smiles and empties the trunk of all the things that he will be showing.

I stand lookout, hoping that the principal doesn't show up.

Biddle Middle . . . Get ready for GUM!

Chapter 10

For over an hour, GUM has been showing the class things from around the world.

He's let them play some musical instruments — African drums, castanets from Mexico, and bagpipes from Scotland.

Now GUM is talking about his latest trip, the one to India.

He's showing slides. Some were taken on the road from New Delhi to Agra, where the Taj Mahal is. It's hard to believe that there were so many animals just walking around . . . cows, camels, elephants, monkeys, pigs . . . and that there were so many villages without buildings like we are used to.

"Here," he says, "are some pictures that may shock you."

There's a gasp in the room when GUM shows pictures of the living conditions in some of the places and talks about the poverty. He shows pictures of kids our own age who are running by the side of his car begging for money to live.

I don't think that I will ever again be able to say that "I'm poor" when my allowance runs out.

GUM also talks about what he finds so beautiful and wonderful about India . . . the colors and textures, the history, the people.

He talks about the marketplaces.

Jonelle Buchanan raises her hand. "Are they like our flea markets?"

"In some ways," GUM says. "Here is a picture of one of the stalls in the market."

It's beautiful . . . filled with boxes of bracelets like the ones that he brought back.

"Don't forget," he says. "You all live here in New Jersey. It's not that far from New York City. There are areas of New York that have Indian food, Indian items. You should all make sure that your parents take you into the city, so that you can visit places like the Indian area, like Little Italy, like Chinatown."

"My parents say that New York City isn't safe," Michelle Hoves says, raising her hand. "Anyway, we have an Indian restaurant in town."

GUM gets a look on his face.

Oh no, I think. I hope that he doesn't go on one of his rantings about how some people in America are so narrow-minded, so unknowing about all of the different groups of people, so unwilling to explore. I hope that he doesn't talk about how "Americanized" some of the restaurants are. Sometimes he says that people are eating "McIndian food" and "McChinese" and "McMexican." He says that we should be willing to try the food the way it really is prepared, not the way we've changed it.

He does go on one of his rants but he lets Michelle know that it isn't her fault or even her parents', because that's probably what they were taught.

GUM looks at the class and asks some questions. "How many of you have visited other states? Other countries? Know people from different groups?"

I look at Mrs. Lipschitz to see how she is reacting to GUM.

She's smiling.

GUM smiles at the class and then hands me a pile of what looks like money.

I look at it.

It's Indian money . . . one hundred rupees on each of the bills.

49

"Skate, would you please pass out one of these to each of your classmates to keep," Gum tells me.

I look at him . . . one hundred rupees!

He explains to all of us, "When that's converted to American money, it's not as much as it seems. It's a little like handing someone from another country one hundred pennies. It may seem like a lot, but it's not. The reason that I want each of you to have one is to remind you that there's a world out there . . . to visit, to learn about, to explore . . . and even if you never actually visit each place, know that there are real people there, ones like you, who care about a lot of the same things we do . . . family, education, survival, having a good time. I would love it if you would keep the money in your wallet, or tape it to a mirror in your room, or put it on your bulletin board."

Leo Nabors raises his hand. "Do you mind if I ask you a question?"

GUM looks at him and smiles. "It depends. You can ask. I'll decide if I want to answer."

Leo says, "How come you don't have to work . . . how come you can just spend your whole life traveling? My parents have to work. Are you rich?"

"Leo," Mrs. Lipschitz says.

GUM looks at her. "That's okay. I bet a lot of you wanted to ask that."

Everyone nods, including Mrs. Lipschitz.

GUM continues. "I don't mind answering that question. I worked hard every day in a regular job for a very long time and made very good money inventing computer programs . . . getting involved early on in the Internet . . . and I still do work. I am an investor . . . and because of the way the world is electronically, I can do that anywhere in the world . . . using phones, computers, faxes — so many inventions that weren't even around when I was your age."

"No phones." Melinda Richard gasps. "I couldn't live without a phone."

GUM laughs. "No . . . there were phones. I'm not that old!"

An announcement comes over the loudspeaker. "Would the person who parked in Principal Poindexter's space please move your car *IMMEDIATELY*!"

I look at GUM.

GUM looks at me.

Another announcement comes over the loudspeaker. "Would the person who parked in Principal Poindexter's space and is going to move it immediately please use the intercom to phone the front office *AT ONCE*."

GUM and I look at each other again.

He's still smiling.

I'm not.

At the end of the period, he's going to be leaving the school, but I'm not.

We can all hear the sound of the microphone being taken from the secretary's hand.

"Now listen," Mr. Poindexter bellows. "I want that car moved right now by the parking spot thief or I'm going to have it towed away. I mean it. I had to park in the custodian's place and that's just not right."

No wonder Mr. Poindexter is so upset.

If he's worried about getting the custodian angry, he may just do something major to get GUM's car, Dr. Livingstone, out of his principal parking space.

Mr. Johanson, the custodian, is very good at making sure that NO ONE parks in his spot.

The second day of school, Mr. Booth, the science teacher, parked in that spot.

When he came back, the entire car was filled with those Styrofoam pieces used for packing. It was so funny watching Mr. Booth trying to clean out his car . . . trying to get all those pieces into garbage bags. (Another teacher had to go to the grocery store to pick up those bags because Mr. Johanson refused to give Mr. Booth any.) For days after that, there were little Styrofoam pieces stuck to Mr. Booth's clothes. One day, he even had some teeny pieces stuck to his ear hair.

I hope that GUM locked Dr. Livingstone's door.

I start to bite my lip.

GUM looks at me and then looks at the class, "It's been great talking with you . . . but I've got to go see a man about a parking space."

Everyone starts to laugh.

Mrs. Lipschitz says, "The class is almost over, I'm sorry to say. This has been one of my most enjoyable days of learning, ever. I hope that you all feel the same way."

The class stands up and applauds.

Then the bell rings and we all start getting ready to go, but no one really wants it all to end.

People just keep standing around, asking GUM questions.

They keep looking at all of the objects that he has brought to us from around the world.

Mrs. Lipschitz whispers something to GUM. He nods, and she goes to the intercom to let them know that the space will soon be free.

After telling them, she holds the phone away from her ear.

It's obvious that someone is not happy . . . and something tells me that it is Mr. Poindexter.

I go over to GUM.

It's so great that he is such a big hit.

He hugs me in front of everyone.

I am a little embarrassed, but only a little. Mostly I am proud, very proud.

Susie comes over and gives him a hug, too.

Normally I wouldn't mind.

Even though GUM isn't really her uncle, we all do things together as a family and she and Aunt Polly are really close to GUM, too.

This time I mind, though.

I want to say, "Why don't you find Kiki's great-uncle and go hug him instead?" but I don't.

The principal's voice comes over the loudspeaker. "I'm serious. I want that car moved or I'm going to call a towing service. I'm starting to count right now . . . one hundred, ninety-nine . . ."

GUM smiles. "I'd better be going now."

"See you tonight." I smile at him.

He leaves.

Susie stands around, telling people how she's gone on trips with us and GUM, that he brings things back for her, too, when he goes on trips.

I think about how when my mom gets really mad at someone, she says, "Now that's gotten on my very last nerve."

Well, that's the way I'm feeling about Susie right now.

She's getting on my very last nerve.

I walk to my next class and everyone comes up and tells me how lucky I am that GUM is my great-uncle, how lucky I am that I get to travel with him.

I feel very lucky . . . and very happy.

Huey, Duey, and Louie come up and ask me to ask GUM if they

can carry his bags on his next trip. Actually, Huey says that, and Duey asks if they can just be packed in his luggage . . . and Louie just quacks.

That reminds me . . . I'm late for industrial arts.

It's time to work on my doofus birdhouse.

Chapter 11

My doofus birdhouse is built, ready to be painted.

I, however, am not ready to paint it.

I haven't even drawn the design for it yet.

This is such a stupid project. At the beginning, we were all given exactly the same plans and we all had to make exactly the same birdhouse. We all did except for Clifford Albright, who glued and nailed one of his sides upside down. He says that he did that intentionally because he wanted to make an open-air attic . . . but I'm not so sure of that. Sometimes Clifford is not AllBright. Anyway, this is like back in grade school, when we were all given the same pictures of Thanksgiving turkeys and told to color them in.

I would rather be working on my cartoon entry for *The Biddle Bulletin*.

I've got a blank piece of paper in front of me and I just don't know what to do.

What if Garth Garrison has already done his cartoon and it's wonderful?

I really want to be on the paper.

I think about Monica Dooley, who also wants to be on the paper.

She wants to be on things because it's going to look good for college applications.

Since kindergarten, Monica Dooley has worried about what is going to look good on her college application. She used to try to organize our playing in the sandbox into a club, the Archaeology

Club. Monica is the youngest of ten kids and there is always some brother or sister in her family worried about getting into college.

This is only sixth grade. I really don't think some college is going to look at our records and be all impressed by what we did our first year at Biddle Middle.

I just really want to be working on the paper, especially on art.

Mr. Ormond, the industrial arts teacher, is walking around the room.

He stops at my desk. "Miss Tate, I don't see any work being done on your birdhouse decoration."

What I really want to say is, "You're not seeing it because I haven't done it, duh." But that would be really rude, so I don't say it . . . I just think it.

"I hear that you are quite a talented artist," Mr. Ormond says. "I'm sure that talent will come in handy even on projects that are not quite to your liking."

Something tells me that he overheard me saying to Liberty, who is in the class, that making the house was "for the birds."

I sigh.

He points to the blank piece of paper and says, "I want to see something by the end of the period."

I think that if I can't figure out what to design, he is going to see something by the end of the period . . . but what he is going to see is that same blank piece of paper.

But I don't say that out loud, either.

Sometimes I think that some students have an entire life going on inside their heads that doesn't come out.

Doodling on the paper, I intentionally break the point of my pencil so that I can get up and go to the sharpener.

I do that so I can look at what everyone else is doing.

It's not that I want to do what someone else is doing, I just want to see some of his or her ideas, see if that can "jump-start" my own brain into being creative.

It's very hard to be creative when you don't care about something.

I go past a table of boys who are designing their birdhouses to look like combat planes and tanks. They are making sounds like, "Vroom, vroom." And, "Ack. Ack."

At another table, Melinda Markham is working hard on her birdhouse. She's drawn a line down the middle and half of the birdhouse looks Victorian and the other half looks like an apartment building. Staring angrily out of a window on the apartment side is a man. There's a cartoon bubble coming out of his mouth saying, "Leave me alone. I am living my new life." The Victorian house has a woman in the window. She's saying, "Your old life has children to support, you swine."

I feel bad for Melinda.

There's a line at the pencil sharpener.

I guess I'm not the only person having trouble with this assignment.

Finally, my pencil gets sharpened and I walk back to my desk.

Liberty is designing her house as a brain and putting up a sign that says, "Only a birdbrain would live here."

I wish that I had thought of that.

I wish that I had thought of anything.

Why is it important to my school life that I know how to make and decorate the outside of a birdhouse?

I doodle on my paper so that it looks like I'm working.

I would rather be in art class or doing my scrapbooking.

I think about GUM and how much fun it was in language arts today and how boring it is in industrial arts.

I wonder what this class would have been like if GUM had visited it.

Maybe he would have talked about "Birdhouses Around the World."

That's it, I think.

I'll design a hotel for traveling birds and decorate it using scrapbooking materials.

Getting out a new piece of paper, I begin.

My bird hotel will be called "Dew Drop Inn . . . the Rest Nest." The front will be the entrance, with carrier pigeons bringing up the luggage. A wise old owl will be at an outside information desk. There will be a large sign in front of the hotel that will say, "Rooms are cheep and cheerful . . ." Another sign will say, "No feather pillows."

There will be a side entrance for the restaurant, which will be called CATCHES . . . which will be short for the early bird CATCHES the worm.

The only thing that I like more than an exciting assignment in school is a boring one that suddenly becomes exciting.

Now if only I can get a great idea for my cartoon.

Chapter 12

Finally, after three more days, scrapbooking saves me . . . again.

First it helped me with the stupid birdhouse, which I hate to admit but I really like a lot now.

Now, it's solved my problems with the cartoon . . . at least I hope that it has!

I've done "A Day in the Life of a Sixth Grader" as a series of scrapbook pages.

I hope that Mrs. Lipschitz likes it. She should, since she's a scrapbooker, too.

I hope that Garth Garrison has a temporary loss of talent so that he turns in a really really bad cartoon.

That sounds so mean that I change my hope.

I hope that Garth Garrison turns in a perfectly wonderful cartoon and that mine is just sooooooooooo much better than his that I become the newspaper artist and art editor.

Actually, it would be perfect if we could both be chosen.

The phone rings.

I hope it's for me.

Dad's still at work.

Mom and Emma are out driving in Mom's new-used car, Wind.

We named it Wind, not because "it moves like the wind" but because it has an annoying little backfire that sounds like someone is breaking wind. (We were going to call it something else, but decided THAT name was a little too gross.)

I think that Emma is going to Caitlin's house.

I hope that this phone call is not for them because then it would be a waste of a run to the phone. It's also a pain if it's for them because I have to write down a message and then remember to tell them about it.

Maybe it's Susie, but I doubt it.

I think that she's over at Kiki's house.

Susie actually tried out for the drama club and got in.

I never knew that she was that interested in drama.

I pick up my smiley face phone. "Hello."

"Hi, Skate."

I recognize GUM's voice immediately.

"Hi, GUM," I say.

"I'm back from the city. Do you have time to come over?" he says.

"I'll be over in a sec." I grin into the phone.

"Just remember to put your name up so that your parents know where you are," he reminds me.

I hang up and hurry over to the wooden board that GUM gave us five Christmases ago.

On the top part of the board, our names are written on individual tags that are kept on hooks.

On the bottom is a long, thin board with hooks. Written on the top of that is, "I'm at GUM's." We move our name tags to that section when we go over to visit GUM's side of the house.

(I think that our house was originally what people call a grandmother house. I guess we could call it an uncle house, but we don't. We just call it home.)

It's another Tate tradition.

I guess I like family traditions.

I move my name to the correct hook and go to GUM's entrance.

GUM looks a little tired.

"Are you okay?" I ask.

He nods. "I've just been running around a lot . . . appoint-ments . . . and some shopping."

There's something about the way he says "shopping" that tells me who is going to get some of what he's bought.

I follow him into the living room and we sit down.

I don't want to do my "What did you bring me?" routine, so I just smile at him.

He smiles back and then hands me a very large plastic shopping bag, which has a bow on it.

I grin at him and then look inside.

It's one of those combo backpack-wheelies.

I am so happy.

There are so many more books and things to carry around in the sixth grade.

My knapsack was weighing me down.

My back was killing me.

This backpack-wheelie is terrific . . . and it's turquoise, one of my favorite colors.

I love that GUM always remembers things like that.

Once I asked him what his favorite color was and he answered, "Plaid."

"It's beauteous," I say. "Thank you so much. I thank you. My back thanks you. Thank you."

"You're welcome." He smiles at me. "Look inside, honey."

I do.

There are gift-wrapped packages inside . . . a lot of them.

"GUM. Wow. This is like Christmas or my birthday."

"Open this one first," GUM says. "Be careful with these."

It's a camera . . . a major camera, not like the little ones that I'm used to having . . . the ones that are one step up from the dispos-ables. This one has a removable lens and everything.

"Oh, thank you." I think about the kind of pictures I will be able to take now . . . close-ups, everything.

He points to another package.

I open the package.

It's a camera case, turquoise.

I smile at him. "GUM . . . this is wonderful . . . but why now?"

". . . just want to . . . now open this." He points to another package.

I grin and rip open the next package.

This one is a camera for use with the computer.

I've always wanted one of these.

Next comes a camera bag for it. This one is black.

"Color-coding," GUM says. "That way you will know which camera is which."

As much as I love everything, I have to say something. "GUM. This is all really expensive. What's going on? Why don't you wait until Christmas? It's only a few months away."

He says, "The other night I was looking at your scrapbooks and I realized how really talented you are . . . and I just want you to have these things."

"You think I'm talented?"

He nods. "Very . . . and I think you will use these things well. A camera gives you a way of looking at and interpreting the world. It's a way to remember."

I think for a minute. "Did you get these for Emma, too?"

He shakes his head. "I got her a video camera. That's more like the way she looks at the world . . . and she'll be able to be a 'film actress' with it. I also bought her an editing program."

I just look at him. This is amazing. This is weird. I know that GUM has a lot, a lot of money and he buys us things and takes us places . . . but this is just so much. I don't get it.

GUM hands me the last package, which was not in the back-pack. It's bigger than the others are.

When I unwrap it, I find an over-the-shoulder traveling bag.

"Look inside," says GUM.

I open it.

It's a smiley face pillow.

"I'll put this on my bed," I say. "Thank you so much."

"I had another idea for it," GUM says.

I sit down to listen.

"I thought, if you like the idea, that you can take it on trips and photograph it wherever you go. That way even if it's one of the times that I can't go on the trip, it will be like I'm there."

Holding the pillow up near his face, I say, "I'm naming him Mr. Smiley Face. You and Mr. Smiley Face look a little alike. I can see the resemblance."

"Thank you." He continues. "It's also a good way to meet people. You can go up to strangers and ask them to hold the pillow in front of their faces. Just be sure that your parents are there when you do that, for safety. It'll be fun."

I say, "I would just be so embarrassed to do that."

He makes a face at me. "Nonsense. It will be fun. Want me to teach you how to do it?"

I giggle and nod.

He picks up the phone.

"Hi, Helen. It's Mort. Is it okay if Skate and I go out for the evening? I'll bring her back after dinner, in time to do her homework."

Obviously my mom is home or on her cell phone and I can tell that she says yes even though she usually doesn't want me to go out on a school night.

"I've finished my homework," I tell GUM. "We can stay out even later."

He shakes his head. And then he grins at me. "I would have tried that, too, when I was your age."

"But I really have finished all the work that I have to hand in," I defend myself.

"And ALL the studying that you could possibly do to prepare yourself?" He looks into my eyes.

"Almost." I just can't lie, especially to him.

GUM fills the cameras with film.

We go out.

I say, "Dr. Livingstone, I presume," and we get into the car and go into town.

While GUM drives, I think about the presents again. GUM does buy us a lot of things and he does take us a lot of places, but he says that he doesn't want to "spoil us." He wants us to know that things are better if we work for them. But all this stuff is definitely "spoiling" me. I'm confused.

"We're here." GUM pulls into a parking space.

He hands me the camera and holds on to Mr. Smiley Face.

GUM is really not afraid of anything.

I watch as he goes up to all sorts of people, smiles, and explains what he wants to do and why.

They smile at him and then at me.

I am very embarrassed at first.

He stops people we know and gets them to pose with Mr. Smiley Face in front of their faces.

He gets people we don't know to do that.

He even has a dog do it.

I see two eighth graders from Biddle Middle School watch as he does this.

I am even more embarrassed, but they come over and ASK to be photographed with Mr. Smiley.

One of the girls says that her little brother, Seth, is in my class and came home and talked about how wonderful it was when GUM came to class. She said that GUM had been to her house once, to play poker with a bunch of other guys.

He asks her who her dad is, and then says, "Oh, yes. He once talked about going white-water rafting. Have him give me a call if he still wants to do it."

Wow . . . GUM knows the dad of an eighth grader.

GUM has me put the pillow in front of my face and stand in the middle, with an eighth grader on either side.

"Smile," he calls out and takes the picture.

I smile even though my face can't be seen behind the pillow.

When the girls ask for a copy of the picture, GUM promises to get one for each of them and to have me deliver it.

We are all having such a good time.

And they talk to me. GUM's right. It's a great way to meet people. But I'm not sure that I can do it without him.

"Skate." GUM looks at his watch and says, "It's time to get some dinner."

Sushi. My favorite.

We sit there and tell each other things.

He tells me about the trip that he's taking next week to Bermuda.

I tell him about my cartoon . . . and how much I want to be on the paper . . . how worried I am that I won't be picked . . . and how scary middle school is.

Then he says, "Skate. You know how much I love you. I don't expect you to be perfect. BUT, I really wish you would get over this. The future is not to be feared but to be explored and celebrated. . . . I really believe that we should be excited by what's just around the corner."

"What if something bad happens?" I bite my lip.

"Deal with it." He shrugs. "And then go on with life."

65

I think about what he has just said and am so glad that he tells me important things.

"GUM," I say. "It's really great that you are spending time here. I miss you when you are traveling for a long time."

"Me too. I miss you and your family a lot when I'm away . . . but you know how much traveling means to me." GUM looks right at me. It's a little embarrassing because I have soy sauce running down my chin. "You know something, Skate? If I'd ever had children, I would have wanted them to be just like you and Emma."

That makes me very happy.

I just grin and think about how glad I am that he is my GUM . . . and how much I will miss him while he is in Bermuda.

I can't wait for him to get back.

Chapter 13

It's **10:45 in the morning** and it's lunchtime for sixth graders at Biddle Middle.

We're eating in the cafetorinasium. The room is used during the day as a cafeteria, an auditorium, and a gymnasium depending on the time of day. So not only is it crowded, not only is the time to eat short, but the room always smells like a combination of hot dogs and gym socks and sweaty bodies.

Susie is still sitting at our table.

Kiki and her group eat lunch at another time. That's because they are all taking a pottery elective that meets at this time.

Susie tried to get into it, but the class was all filled up.

It doesn't make me feel great to know that she would be somewhere else if she could be but because she can't, she's still sitting with us.

I wonder what will happen if I get to be part of *The Biddle Bulletin*.

I'm just about positive that I won't feel any differently about my friends.

I've known Susie since we were little and neither of us is like we were when we were babies. We've changed a lot. But we've always changed in ways that the other got used to . . . now it seems different.

Susie takes a bite of her french fry. "I'm going to flunk art. I just know it. I can't believe that you wanted to take it so much and didn't get it and I did. They should have let us switch."

I sigh and think about how we went to Guidance and tried to switch. It would have been so easy. Both classes take place on the same days, at the same time. We both wanted the class that the other one had.

Mr. Dench, the guidance counselor, wouldn't let us switch. He said that if we could do that, then everyone could, and what would that do to the scheduling process. That sounded so guidance counselor-like. We didn't come in for guidance, we came in for help.

"Susie. It'll be okay. You're not so bad," I say, trying to make her feel better. "You do a good job on your scrapbooks."

She shrugs. "That's different. That's fun. I can decorate things having to do with me and with things that I like . . . and anyway, you know that I don't even care about scrapbooking as much as I used to. There's other stuff I'd rather do."

That bothers me. The Happy Scrappys are a tradition and a lot of fun and I want Susie to stay, even if she doesn't like it as much.

I don't want middle school to change anything.

At least she's still sitting at our lunch table.

"Enough about stupid art class!" Susie says. "Did you hear? Aaron Dunham and Tracey Gregory broke up."

I shake my head. "Susie. I don't even know who they are. Why should I care about that?"

Susie looks at me and sighs. "They are just two of the most important people in the eighth grade. Really, Skate . . . you should take more of an interest in these things."

"Why?" I ask, really wanting to know.

She sighs again. "It's important to know what's happening in the school, to be part of it. Let me help you with this . . . Aaron is president of the eighth-grade class, and Tracey is one of the best gymnasts in the state . . . AND they've been going together since sixth grade . . . but then Krissy Conroy moved to town and started flirting with Aaron and . . . the rest is history."

"Susie." I giggle. "History is World War II, Abraham Lincoln, Martin Luther King, Jr., the Lewis and Clark expedition."

She looks at me as if I'm hopeless. "You just don't know what's really important. We're in middle school now. Things are different."

I look at my cousin and wonder. I wonder if I'm angry at her for acting like this. I wonder if we will always be friends, as well as cousins.

I hope so.

Sometimes I wonder.

Sometimes I worry.

Daisy joins us.

She puts her tray down and spills some of her french fries.

Then she opens her juice and spills it on top of the french fries.

She picks up a soggy fry. "Yummers. Cranberry juice fries. Want one?"

We shake our heads.

"Guess what?" she says. "I'm going to have a rock-and-roll birthday party. All of the girls and boys will wear clothes from the ancient 1950s and we'll play that music. I decided that today in math class."

"Great," Susie says. "That will be soooooooooo fun."

I say, "Terrific," and then I think about it. "Daisy. This is September. Your birthday isn't until February."

"I know when my birthday is." She giggles. "You know that I like to plan ahead . . . and math was very boring, so I spent the time figuring everything out."

She opens her notebook and shows us what she did during math class. There's the guest list page. She's numbered to fifty, but there are only nineteen names on the page.

"It's early in the year," she says. "We'll know more people by then."

She's also worked out the menu, the music, and what she'll wear.

The bell rings.

Twenty-two minutes for lunch . . . by the time we get through the lunch line, it's almost time to go.

Some of the kids start eating as soon as the food goes on the tray, and by the time they get to the cashier, their trays are practically empty. It's the honor system, and the kids are supposed to tell exactly what they took. There is this one cafeteria worker who can smell your breath and figure out exactly what you ate on the way through the line. . . . She can also tell when was the last time you brushed your teeth.

I rush to class.

It's language arts, with Mrs. Lipschitz.

We're reading *Out of the Dust* by Karen Hesse.

I really like it.

We spend the period talking about what life must have been like during the Depression.

I look down at the postcard that I am using as a bookmark.

It's from GUM.

He's gotten to Bermuda, is having a great time, and wishes we were there. He says that he'll be back in about a week.

I can't wait to show him the Mr. Smiley Face pictures that we took on the day he gave me the cameras.

The bell rings.

As I leave, Garth and I bump into each other.

I sort of smile at him.

He sort of smiles at me.

Today is the day that we find out who is on the newspaper.

What if I don't get chosen?

What if I have to sit in classes, look at Garth, and know that he got chosen and I didn't?

In history, we are studying the Middle Ages.

Maybe Garth and I should duel for the job.

I can just see it now. . . . His science fiction warriors versus my scrapbook pages and drawings . . . I just hope that the sticker is mightier than the sword.

My stomach is doing flip-flops.

It's so hard to sit in classes and act interested when all I really care about is being on the newspaper. Even though I say that it doesn't matter, it does.

Finally, it's the end of the day and the announcements come on.

The bell rings and it's time to go to "the Press Room," which is really Mrs. Lipschitz's classroom.

There are a lot of kids there.

I hate this.

Mrs. Lipschitz has posted the results on the bulletin board, and kids are trying to get close enough to see.

I watch as Mindy Farley leaves the room, trying not to cry.

Huey, Duey, and Louie waddle in.

I watch as some of the kids sit down in seats and some leave.

Some leave like Mindy, trying not to cry.

A few look like they are crying.

Some look like they don't care . . . but I bet they do.

I am trying to get up enough nerve to go look at the list.

Huey goes up, looks at the list, and then comes back to Duey and Louie.

He does not look happy.

He does not look like everything is "ducky."

Huey looks at his friends and says, "Let's go. I didn't make it. Duey didn't make it. Louie, you made it . . . but let's just get out of here."

Louie grins. "I made it? I made it!"

"Yes." Huey frowns. "You did . . . but so what? Weren't you listening? Duey and I didn't make it. So let's go. We're a team. Teams do things together."

Louie looks at Huey and then at Duey.

"Come on, Louie," Duey says. "Let's go practice for the basketball tryouts."

Louie gets out of his seat but just stands there. He looks at his friends and then he looks at the kids who are sitting down. "Look guys . . . I really want to write sports. You just tried out because I said it was something I wanted to do. You wrote your articles at lunch."

"We're a team," Huey says.

Louie looks at him.

Huey continues. "You're either part of the D.D.T. or you're not." Huey looks very annoyed. "Let's get quacking."

Duey quacks.

Then Louie quacks.

I feel really bad when Louie quacks. He's giving in.

Louie picks up his books and then looks around the room.

He puts his books down again. "Huey. Duey. You two are better basketball players than I am. What if you make the team and I don't? Will you give up being on the team?"

Duey immediately tells him, "We'll all make the team. We'll coach you."

Huey says, "And if you don't make it, you can still come to the games and watch us play."

Louie stands quietly for a minute and then says, "I am going to come to the games and watch . . . and then write about it. I'm going to be on the paper."

He sits down again.

I want to applaud.

Louie says, "Don't be mad. I'll see you guys later."

"Not if we see you first." Huey turns and walks out.

Duey looks at Huey leaving, then at Louie, and he shrugs. "See you later."

Louie just sits there.

I feel like I've just watched something major happen.

Looking around the room, I see Heather being angry at Eric.

She's just found out that she's not on the paper and she's breaking up with him.

I watch as Garth goes over to the list.

He turns around, smiling.

And then he sits down.

That's it, I think.

I've got to try to get out of here with my head up.

I take a deep breath, look straight ahead, and head out the door.

I'm halfway down the hall when I hear someone yell, "Skate."

It's Garth Garrison.

I guess that I have to go back and say, "Congratulations."

I just wanted to leave.

I didn't think that he was the kind of kid who is a gloater.

I walk back toward the classroom.

Garth walks toward me.

In my head I practice. "Congratulations, Garth."

I hope that I can say it without crying.

In less than a minute, we are standing close, facing each other.

"Garth." I look at him. "Congratulations."

He smiles shyly. "Thanks."

And then he says, "Skate. Congratulations to you, too."

I just look at him. "What do you mean?"

He grins. "You didn't look at the list, did you?"

I shake my head. "I figured you got chosen."

"I did." He nods. "But so did you. We both got chosen."

If I were the kind of person who fainted, I would faint right now. My legs feel a little wobbly and I hold on to a nearby locker.

Garth continues. "It says that an art editor will be chosen later . . . but I don't care about that. You can be editor. I just want to do the art."

I grin at him and nod. "Me, too . . . well, maybe I would like to be the art editor, too. We'll see."

Mrs. Lipschitz comes out. "The meeting's about to start."

Garth and I walk into the room.

I am one very happy person.

Chapter 14

I **can't believe that it's October.**
I can't believe how much homework there is in middle school.

I can't believe how much has happened in just about a month.

The doorbell rings. One long and two short ones . . . that's Susie's signal.

She's still coming to the Happy Scrappy meetings.

I used to be very happy when I heard her doorbell signal . . . now I'm not so sure.

Susie comes in. For years, it was like we all lived in the same house even though we didn't.

When I was really little and Susie and Aunt Polly had moved to our block, it was confusing. Sometimes I called Aunt Polly "Mom" and my mom "Mom." Susie did the same.

When Susie was very little, sometimes she called my father "Uncle Dad." It was kind of weird, but Susie's dad died when she was four and then she and her mom moved here from California. So my dad is the closest thing to a dad she's ever had.

Susie walks in.

Her hair is blue . . . bright blue . . . electric blue.

I'm not sure if I love it or hate it.

I wonder what my parents would say if I did that to my hair.

I wonder what they will say about her hair.

I just stare at her with my mouth open.

She grins and shakes her hair around. "Fun, huh?! It washes out in about three shampoos."

"When did you do it?" I manage to close my mouth to allow for speech.

"Last night," she says. "Slumber party at Gwen Nevele's."

Gwen Nevele is a friend of Kiki's, one of the kids who went to one of the other elementary schools, Clara Barton Elementary. She's part of a whole group from there who still hangs out together. She's in my math class but I really don't know her. Obviously Susie does.

When we were little, Susie and I did practically everything together, told each other everything.

She didn't even tell me that she was invited to the slumber party.

"Do you like it?" she asks.

For a minute I think she's talking about how it's changed between us and I almost say "No." Then I realize that she's talking about her hair color.

I nod. "Do you?"

She smiles. "Yes. Not forever, but for now. It's going to be fun going into school on Monday. Gwen's hair is strawberry. Kiki's is lime green. Shoranda's is fluorescent yellow. Betina's is orange."

When they walk down the hall, I wonder if they are going to look like packages of Kool-Aid.

"Would you take a picture so that I can put it in my scrapbook?" she asks. "When I got home, Mom wasn't too happy about this, so I didn't ask her. She's calmed down now, but I didn't want to push my luck."

I wondered what Aunt Polly thought about it.

Susie continues. "She made me promise that I wouldn't do anything extreme without permission . . . no piercings, no tattoos."

I take out my new camera and take a picture and then go in for a close-up.

As Mrs. Barker, the Scout leader who got us started scrapbooking, used to say, "Everything's a photo-op."

I personally don't think that *everything* is a photo opportunity, but this definitely is.

The doorbell rings.

I answer it and leave the door open for the others to come in.

It's Liberty.

As she walks in, everyone in her mother's car leans out, waves . . . her mom, her little brothers, Austin and Troy.

It's a little embarrassing for Liberty, but her parents named their kids for the places they were first "started." The Davis family has traveled to Texas and upstate New York. I hope that they never spend the night in Nutley, New Jersey . . . Nutley Davis. I don't think any kid should have to be named that.

Liberty's name came from a town in New York. . . . Her parents are always saying part of the Gettysburg Address . . . the part that goes, "Conceived in liberty and dedicated to . . ." They always laugh a lot. Liberty always blushes a lot.

During the Pledge of Allegiance, kids sometimes ask who justice is because of the "for liberty and justice for all" part.

Some of the boys at school sometimes look at her and yell, "Give me liberty or give me death," and then they pretend to die. Liberty always ignores them.

Daisy arrives and immediately trips and drops all of her supplies all over the floor.

We all help her pick them up and then we get to work . . . and we talk.

We all talk a lot.

I find out that Cindy Cooper is quitting soccer because she gets a manicure every week now and she doesn't want to ruin her nails.

Aaaarg . . .

The only time I ever got a manicure, I had pictures of soccer balls airbrushed onto my nails.

I find out that Barbie Fenton saw Mr. Bertonetti, the phys ed teacher, and Miss Miller, the French teacher, at the Cineplex at a mall four towns away. Barbie was visiting a friend from camp and she swears that she and her friend were sitting just two rows behind the teachers. She counted the times the teachers kissed each other . . . seven times during the coming attractions and eleven times during the movie.

We talk about the activities that we are joining.

Daisy is in ceramics club and in current events club. That's in addition to the confirmation class that she's taking at her church.

Susie wants to be a cheerleader . . . in her spare time.

Emma says, "I can't wait until I get to middle school."

We all smile at her.

Even though at school, the eighth graders are the big shots and sixth graders are the "little shots," we still seem very important to a fourth grader.

We work on our pages and look at what the others are doing. It's kind of like we were at some of the things, too.

Finally, cleanup time and The Happy Scrappys leave . . . except for those who actually live in the house, Emma and me.

It's been a fun day.

Dinnertime and then family game time.

Tonight we are playing one of our favorites, Scrabble.

I have just gotten fifty-seven points for the word "fixed."

I am very proud.

The phone rings.

My father answers it.

He listens for a minute.

"Yes. This is Jim Tate."

"Yes. He is."

Then my father is very quiet.

Then he asks, "What?"

He listens and then asks, "When? How?"

We are all very quiet.

We can't tell what the call is about but we can tell that it is something that is very major.

My dad puts down the phone and starts to cry.

I've never seen my dad cry.

Mom goes up to him quietly and puts her arm around his waist.

We all stay quiet until he can say something.

And then he says something that we don't want to hear. "GUM is dead."

Chapter 15

I **look at the sympathy cards** that people have sent us for the last two weeks.

I know that people mean well, that they just want to make us feel better, but the cards and notes don't say what really happened.

GUM is no longer with us. That sounds like he's gone on another trip.

GUM has passed. That sounds like he's just gotten test results back.

GUM has gone to meet his maker. That sounds like he's some kind of robot going back to meet his inventor.

GUM is in a far better place. That sounds like he's at a resort.

I think people should just say it.

GUM is dead.

He is dead.

I am so sad.

I am so angry.

I am so upset.

I love him so much.

So now do I have to say I loved him so much?

And if it happened to him, could it happen to other people I love? Like my dad? Like my mom?

It's two weeks since it happened and I'm finding out things . . .

Things like my mom and dad knew that GUM had found out that he had a heart condition. That's why he had all those appointments in New York. My mom says that they even tried to convince him to slow down, to stay here for a while.

He told them that he just wanted to continue to live "normally," that the doctor was trying to control it with medicine.

"Normally" for GUM wasn't like "normally" for a lot of people.

I'm just so mad.

Didn't he love us enough to change the way he was living so that he would live longer?

It's all so hard.

When it first happened, lots of people in my class came up to me and told me how sorry they were.

Now, it's like it's old news and no one says anything about it anymore, but every day I feel it and miss him. Now it's not every minute of the day, but it happens. I'll be doing something and then I think, Wait until I write to GUM and tell him. He'll love hearing about this. Then I remember that he won't get the message, that it will go to the dead letter office. DEAD. There's that word again. But it's not the letter that's DEAD, it's GUM.

"Skate," my mom calls up the stairs. "We're waiting."

I look in the mirror.

I'm wearing the outfit that I wore the day that GUM took Emma, Susie, and me to a Broadway show. That day he tap-danced down the street and then took us to a jewelry store, where we each got to pick out a present.

I put on the amethyst necklace that I got. It's on a silver chain, with one stone on it. I love it.

I'm wearing my black pants and turquoise sweater.

Turquoise was his favorite color, too.

Just before I go downstairs, I pick up Mr. Smiley Face, the pillow that GUM gave me.

Now I know why he gave me all those presents without waiting for Christmas.

I throw Mr. Smiley Face on the floor.

GUM knew that he might not be alive at Christmas.

That makes me so mad.

That makes me so sad.

I pick up Mr. Smiley Face again and hug him.

If we're going to have a family memorial service for GUM, then I want Mr. Smiley Face there with me.

I bet if there was a way for Mr. Smiley Face to not be smiling now, he would be crying.

I go downstairs.

Mom, Dad, and Emma are waiting.

There's also a framed picture of GUM on the table with a little candle in front of it.

I can feel my tears starting.

I clutch my pillow and try not to cry.

My dad speaks. "When GUM talked to me about this, he told me that if anything happened, he did not want a funeral or a big memorial service. He also said that he realized that it would be important for just us, his family, to acknowledge his death, but that he would like it if we had a celebration of his life."

My mom sniffles.

My dad puts his hand on her shoulder.

I can't believe that they both knew about GUM's heart condition and didn't warn us about it.

It's not fair that grown-ups get to keep important secrets from their kids.

Dad continues. "So even though many people wanted to have a memorial service for him, we're going to honor his wishes and do it his way. He said that it would be okay for each of us to mention one memory and say something about him that would continue to be part of your life. He said that that way, it would be as if he is still in the world."

My mom sniffles again. "That was just like GUM, to try to plan everything out, to want to have it done the way that HE wanted it to be."

She shakes her head, looks at my father and smiles and says, "Some days he could drive me crazy, but I really loved your uncle."

Dad smiles back. "Even though sometimes he called you The D.F.?"

Mom smiles at my dad. "Yes, even though he sometimes called me The D.F. . . . Remember when I accidentally burned the fish that had been caught when we went camping? GUM was going to have us go into the woods and find berries for us to eat for dinner. I took the keys to the car and went out and found the nearest McDonald's and brought back dinner. Then I told him that he could forage for food his way and I would do it my way."

"Then he said that you were not only a D.F., but an F.F.F. — a Fast-Food Forager." I start to laugh.

Sometimes GUM and Mom didn't agree.

It's fun to remember that, because even though they didn't always agree, it was obvious that they loved each other.

Dad says, "Now I think that each of us should tell the memory that we want to share about GUM."

My mom says, "I'll start . . . but I have two memories that I want to share. I know GUM said one, but you know that GUM and I didn't always agree and I didn't always do what he wanted me to do."

She smiles. "If GUM were here right now, you know that he would grump a lot about my not following directions."

We nod.

"And you also know that I would then remind him that he wasn't very good at following directions, either." She nods back.

We nod again.

My dad says, "In some ways, I think that you and GUM were more alike than he and I were."

My parents look at each other and smile.

Mom continues. "So here goes . . . I will always remember that GUM lived with a sense of adventure. Since I grew up in a family that 'stayed put,' and never went anywhere, GUM let me see that there is a whole wide world out there."

My mom said, "I will also always remember GUM's extraordinary kindness and generosity. Although he wasn't really related to Aunt Polly and Susie, GUM was so helpful when Uncle Bob was killed in that car accident. And I know that there are many other people and many organizations that were helped by your uncle."

My dad clears his throat. "Mort Tate was an extraordinary man. He was smart, kind, and charitable. He loved us all very much. When my dad died, I was only fifteen, and Mort became like a father to me. He was my adviser. He was my friend. I can't imagine what our lives will be like without him."

I think about how Dad's dad was dead at forty and now GUM is dead at fifty-seven. I think about how I once overheard my dad say that the men in his family "have bad tickers" and that's why he is so careful about eating right and exercising. I feel sick thinking about that. Dad was only four years older than I am when his dad died. Dad is only four years younger than his dad was when his dad had the heart attack and died. Until now, I never thought about stuff like this. Now I don't know if I can ever stop thinking about it and worrying.

My dad continues. "One of my favorite memories is the time GUM was flying back from a rafting trip early because he had promised Skate that he would be in time for her kindergarten concert. There was a terrible storm. His plane was grounded and he couldn't make it back in time. So that night, I took my cell phone to the concert and called GUM's phone while he sat in an airport lounge. He listened to her entire concert, just as he had promised her that he would."

That memory makes me smile. Now that I'm older, I know what a big deal that is, but back then I thought it was totally normal.

Emma says, "What I remember about . . ." and that's as far as she gets. She puts her hands in front of her face and starts to cry.

That makes me cry.

Taking a deep breath, she begins again. "I love everything about GUM and I don't want to talk about him like he's dead."

We all sit quietly.

I think about what she's just said.

I don't want to talk about him like he's dead, either. But he is dead.

Sometimes it hurts more when I think he's alive and then I remember that he isn't. It's like he's died again.

So I decide to share the memory that I have chosen.

I talk about the day that he took just me to the Metropolitan Museum. That was the day I told him how much I wanted to be an artist. It was one of the first times that I had ever said it out loud. He said that I already was an artist . . . that I was creating and developing myself.

I'm not sure that GUM saying that each of us could give one example was enough. We could go on for hours.

I just wish that he were here to hear it.

I just wish that he were here to comfort us in our loss . . . but if he were here, there would be no reason to have to comfort us.

My father says, "Now there is one more thing that GUM wanted us to do."

Our parents look at each other and then my father continues. "As you know, Mom and I went into New York City on Wednesday."

We nod.

Emma and I went over to Aunt Polly's house after school that night and had dinner there.

It was a little like it used to be B.K. (That means Before Kiki.)

My father continues. "We had to meet with GUM's lawyer, Mr. Rhoades, about GUM's will."

GUM's will . . . I didn't think about that.

"Your uncle left a great deal of his money to organizations that meant a lot to him . . . charities that help people and the environment."

"Go, GUM." I hug GUM in my mind.

My mom pulls out a video. "GUM wanted us to watch this as a family."

I wonder what the film is.

GUM always loved a lot of foreign films, the kind with subtitles.

I don't like those a lot.

I'm always afraid that if I blink, I'm going to miss something important.

So I hope that it's not one of those, because my eyes already hurt from crying.

We sit down.

"GUM filmed this in his lawyer's office shortly after he got the doctor's report. He left it there with instructions for us in case of his death." My dad's voice sounds sad when he says "death." "Your mom and I have already seen it. Now we want to share it with you."

We sit down in the Tate Family Sandwich.

That's what we call it . . . a parent on each side, two kids in the middle.

The video starts.

It's GUM. "If you are watching this, it means that I am no longer here on earth . . . and I want to remind you, I don't want to be in the earth either. Jim, you know that I don't want to be buried. I want to be cremated and my ashes to be scattered over the ocean near San Francisco."

Emma and I both go, "Oooooooooooooh."

I don't want to think about my uncle being burned up.

GUM continues. "I know that you girls are going, 'Ooooooooooh,' but stop that . . . it's not so bad."

We look at each other and laugh.

That is so GUM!

"Now there's a lot of things in the will for the adults to look at . . . so I won't discuss all of that now. What I do want to do now is ask the four of you to do me a favor."

Anything, I think, anything for you.

"I've given instructions to my lawyer, Arthur Rhoades. He'll handle all of the legal things. Just for your information, he is a very good lawyer, but my favorite thing about him is that I could give him a nickname . . . Dusty . . . get it??? Dusty Rhoades."

GUM chuckles.

I often read old stories where someone chuckles. I hardly ever hear anyone "chuckle." But GUM does.

GUM says, "I've always hoped that I was going to be around for a long time, to take you to places that I've loved and to go to places with you where I have never been. Well, now I won't be able to do that . . . but I would love it if you would continue to travel as much as possible. I have made out a list of places that I wanted to show you, that I wanted us to discover together. To that end, I have left a specific amount of money that will allow you to travel. While I don't want to be a dictator about this . . . I know, D.F., that you think I could sometimes be a dictator . . ." He smiles when he says that.

We all look at my mom, who nods at the TV.

GUM continues. "I would be so happy if you would travel, but not as tourists. I would like it if you would learn something about the places, meet people there, take time to see why that place is important. I want you to expand your horizons, to not be afraid, to not be stuck in one place."

We all look at one another.

GUM used to talk with us about this a lot.

"So," he says, "talk about this as a family. Know that you can use the money to include Polly and Susie when you want to do so. If you decide to use the money allotted to you for travel, it will fulfill one of my greatest wishes. Think of this as an adventure . . . you're the United Tates of America . . . and very importantly, know that I love you lots."

Each of us say "love you lots" at the same time.

Just as the video comes to the end, GUM says, "And by the way, Jim, enjoy Dr. Livingstone and don't forget to get his oil changed."

The video is over.

We all look at one another.

"Your mother and I have already discussed this," Dad says. "We feel that it's a terrific idea. It will be wonderful to be able to travel without worrying about how we are going to be able to afford it . . . and to know that it is something that was very important to GUM."

Emma and I agree.

"One more thing," my mom says. "Your dad and I have discussed the fact that GUM would not have liked it if we used the money in a lavish way . . . so we want to budget our trips and make a charity donation with whatever money is left over at the end of the year from the travel budget."

"There goes the limo." I hold up Mr. Smiley Face, pretending that he is saying that. "And I guess that the yacht is out of the question, too."

I can't help it.

If I don't say something funny soon, I may just explode from sadness.

My mom starts to laugh.

So does my dad.

Actually, Dad chuckles.

For a second, he sounds like GUM.

We talk about what it will be like to do a lot of traveling as a family, about how GUM has left a list not only of places but of things that he would like us to do in each one. . . . There are historical places like Plymouth, and Washington, D.C., and Williamsburg. . . . He also suggested things to do — going on wagon trains, canal boat rides, getting to really know this country, even visiting foreign countries.

Our parents already think it's a great idea.

Emma and I quickly agree to the plan.

There's really no need for discussion about this.

GUM wanted us to do this.

It is something that we want to do.

The United Tates of America . . . that's us.

Chapter 16

Mom keeps saying, "Life goes on."

She's right. She's very sad when she says it, but she's right.

It does.

But it doesn't go on in the same way, although some of the things ARE like they were before.

Daisy is coming over so that we can make cookies for tomorrow's sixth-grade bake sale.

That's good, because I need some things to be the same when it feels like some things are so different.

It's just not fair.

Dad keeps saying, "Life isn't fair. You have to learn that. It's just life."

I'm eleven years old.

That's not something that I wanted to learn, not yet, maybe not ever.

The doorbell rings.

It's Daisy.

She's carrying a bag filled with baking supplies.

We go into the kitchen.

Emma's already in there.

Susie's not coming. She's going to bake something with her new friends.

I know that it's mean to think, but I hope that whatever they bake burns.

Liberty can't come because she has to baby-sit for her little brothers.

She and her grandmother are going to bake brownies tonight.

Even though Emma is not a sixth grader, she wants to be part of the baking . . . partly because she likes to bake and partly because it makes her feel like she's practically a sixth grader herself.

Tomorrow's bake sale is the first of a lot of moneymaking things that the sixth graders are going to be doing. That's because at the end of the year, we're going on a class trip, and the more money we earn as a class, the less money we each have to pay.

Daisy takes out icing tools.

She also takes out her camera.

My camera is already out.

It's a scrapbooking thing.

We take out two rolls of cookie dough.

I make a suggestion. "Let's put some cookie dough on the side and save it so that we can eat it raw while the cookies are baking."

Both Emma and Daisy think that this is a wonderful suggestion.

I'm glad that my mom is up in her study working, because she thinks it is bad to eat cookie dough.

Personally I don't understand why it's so bad. It's not like we're going to stand in the hot sun and dough is going to turn into huge cookies inside of us.

Daisy holds up a spoonful of the batter and yells, "Batter up."

Then she lowers the spoon and says, "Batter down the hatches."

"That's BATTEN down the hatches, not batter down the hatches," I tell her.

"Whatever." She grins.

I pick up a spoon, fill it with the goop, and push it at her, going, "Baaaaa, baaaaa, baaaaa."

She just looks at me and rolls her eyes.

"What am I?" I ask.

"A lunatic?" she answers.

"No." I grin at her. "I'm a baaaaaaaaaattering ram." I push the spoon at her again.

I'm not even sure what a battering ram is, but right now it makes a good pun . . . and I like good puns.

I think that's because my entire family likes to joke around with language . . . and because GUM always loved to pun.

Emma looks at us like we are maniacs. "It's dough . . . not batter. Cookies are made with dough. Cakes are made with batter. Duh."

Daisy holds up the tube of sugar cookie dough. "I hope that we sell all of the cookies. It takes a lot of cookie dough to make dough — the money kind!"

We make the cookie shapes.

Finally, the first group of cookies goes into the oven and we sit down for lunch.

"Guess what," Emma tells Daisy. "We're going to Plymouth, Massachusetts, over the teachers convention weekend . . . four days."

Daisy looks at me. "You didn't tell me."

I nod. "We just decided last night."

"Guess what?" Emma asks.

"GUM left a will and we get to travel all over the country. This will be our first trip," Emma says. "Isn't that great?"

Daisy nods.

"Emma," I say, "Dad said that we aren't supposed to talk a lot about the will."

"Oooooops." Emma puts her hand in front of her mouth.

Daisy says, "I promise I won't tell anyone . . . cross my heart and hope to die."

"DON'T SAY THAT," Emma yells.

Daisy and I both look at Emma.

She looks terrified. "Take that back."

Daisy says, "You mean you want me to tell people?"

Emma shakes her head. "No . . . don't tell. And I mean take back the other thing that you said."

Daisy says, "You mean 'cross my . . .'?"

"Yes," Emma yells. "Don't ever say that again."

I think about the last time that Emma asked someone to say that.

It was GUM.

Poor Emma.

What a terrible thing to remember.

I just don't know what to say to her.

"Emma," I say.

"I don't want to talk about it." She pounds on some cookie dough.

The timer rings.

I decide to pretend that everything is okay.

We pull out the cookies.

While we are decorating them, I tell Daisy a little bit about what my parents said about the will.

Emma quietly decorates her cookies.

"You know how much GUM loved to travel?" I start.

Daisy nods.

"Well, he did leave us money to travel. Dad and Mom say that there are a whole lot of other things that we are supposed to do on the road . . . we each have to keep journals . . . and each of us has to start a souvenir collection of something . . . and I am supposed to scrapbook. And they said that there's a lot more to the will."

Daisy thinks for a minute. "Wow. Does this mean that your family is rich now? Wow."

I'm not real comfortable about that question.

I don't know.

Mom and Dad didn't say.

I think that this is another time that they aren't going to tell us everything.

I think about the time when Mom's car died and I wished that we had lots of money.

I've never told anyone, but I wish that I had never never wished for that.

I think that MAYBE now we do have lots of money, but only because GUM is dead.

I wish that I had never made that wish.

Maybe if I had never made that wish, GUM would still be alive today.

It's very quiet for a few minutes and then Daisy leans over with her spatula. There is chocolate icing on it.

She paints a beard on me.

I paint one on her.

We get Emma, too.

Soon all of us are laughing.

The cookies are decorated.

And so are we.

Chapter 17

It's party time.

The first *Biddle Bulletin* of the school year has been distributed.

It's the very first *Biddle Bulletin* that I've ever worked on . . . and I am so happy! I love working on the school paper.

Usually the paper is four pages long, but for the first issue, there are six whole pages.

That means that there was no problem including both Garth's and my comic strips.

Mrs. Lipschitz says that in the future there's a chance there will be only one cartoon or comic strip but that some of the articles may need illustrations.

Garth and I have both shown our own ideas of "A Day at Biddle Middle."

He's drawn a superhero, Bidlothian, who has been turned into Biddleboy. Because of a terrible spell, he must leave most of his superhero powers home and travel through eons and galaxies to become a student at Biddle Middle School. The spell, wished on him by Elfadoodle the Elder, turns Biddleboy into the lowest of the low, a sixth grader who has trouble opening his locker, who can't remember to bring lunch money, who is too shy to ask for the bathroom pass. Even with all that plaguing Biddleboy, he is expected to defend Biddle Middle from all evil, including potpie lunches, and clean up all of the mold in lockers, gym and regular.

Biddleboy is the kind of thing that Garth's been doodling since second grade . . . but this one looks really professional.

My comic strip looks very good, too, but very different.

Scrapbooked . . . funny . . . kind of sweet.

The reason that I did the insides of lockers was to show the different kinds of sixth graders at the school.

Our choices are so different.

I wonder if it's a boy-girl thing or it's just that Garth and I are very different kinds of artists.

I look at *The Biddle Bulletin*.

It looks terrific.

My name is even on the masthead:

CO-ART DIRECTORS — GARTH GARRISON, SARAH KATE TATE

I wish that it could have said Skate, but Mrs. Lipschitz said that nicknames aren't allowed on the masthead.

My comic strip, however, is signed SKATE Tate.

That's great.

There's a knock on the door.

It opens.

It's Heather. "May I please speak with Eric?"

"Tell her I'm not here," Eric says.

No one tells her that he's not here, because she can see him standing there.

Heather continues to stand by the door.

She really hates to miss a party.

Mrs. Lipschitz walks up to Eric, puts her hand on his shoulder, and whispers something to him.

He shrugs and then goes over to the door and goes into the hall with Heather.

Mrs. Lipschitz says, "Let's continue passing out the cake."

We do.

In a minute, Eric comes back in.

He doesn't look too happy, but Heather isn't with him.

Then Eric takes a piece of cake.

I think about how GUM used to say about certain things, "Well, that really takes the cake!"

GUM's not here to say that anymore. He's not here to see *The Biddle Bulletin*. He's not here to see my scrapbook cartoon.

"Girls," Eric says.

I don't think that it's fair for Eric to act like all girls are like Heather.

I think about how I've never even gone out on a date . . . and how, even if I ever do, GUM will never know about it.

Then I think about how maybe I'll never go out on a date and how GUM will never know that, either.

He won't know if I'm dating. He won't know if I'm not dating. He won't know when I make the honor roll. He won't know anything about me ever again and I won't know anything about him ever again.

I hate it. I hate being sad all of a sudden when I was so happy just a minute ago.

That happens a lot since GUM died . . . and I don't like the feeling.

I don't like not being able to go next door and talk to him about anything.

I didn't like it when he was away and I wanted to go next door and talk to him and he wasn't there because he was traveling.

At least then, I knew he was coming back.

Everything seemed much easier when I was a little kid.

My life really could be a set of kids' books . . . first *Skate Tate at Biddle Middle* . . . and *Skate Tate Without a Date* . . . *Skate Tate Without a Great-Uncle*.

GUM really was a great uncle!

My brain is filled with so many things at once.

There are quacking sounds coming from outside the doorway.

It's Huey and Duey. "Feed the ducks. Feed the ducks. The ducks are hungry."

It took a while but they made up with Louie.

I was actually there when they made up. It happened while they were standing on the lunch line.

I overheard Louie saying, "The Donald Duck Trio should not be fighting . . . best friends not getting along is absolutely 'fowl.'"

Huey and Duey looked at each other, then they looked at Louie, and then they each took a chicken tender off his lunch tray.

Then they all quacked and flapped their wings . . . I mean arms.

Then they all ate a chicken tender, which with the way our cafeteria makes it should be called a chicken tough.

Very strange. The "ducks" eat chicken. That seems cannibalistic to me.

Huey, Louie, and Duey are a little weird.

When Louie is working on the paper, though, he's like a real person.

He's a good writer.

His article was about trying out for sports and not making it.

Mrs. Lipschitz said that Louie "wrote a very sensitive, articulate article."

When he is with Huey and Duey, though, he turns into a different person. (Well, actually he turns into a duck.)

Huey and Duey quack again and then say, "Duckys want a cake."

Mrs. Lipschitz goes over to the door and says, "The cake is for those who worked hard on the paper."

I start to giggle.

Mrs. Lipschitz sounds like the Little Red Hen.

Huey and Duey leave.

. . . But they don't leave without one last quack.

Eric and the other eighth graders are looking at the paper, making comments about things they like and things that they don't like. Some of the seventh graders who were on the paper last year join in.

The sixth graders are not included in the same way.

We're the new kids.

When I am in eighth grade, I'm going to try to remember to talk more to the sixth graders.

Mrs. Lipschitz calls out, "Announcement."

We all listen.

"I want you to know that I'm very proud of you. First issue. New mixture of students working on the paper. You've made a fine start." She smiles at us. "We have the makings of a really terrific team. I have heard nothing but good things about the paper."

We all applaud ourselves.

Then everyone goes back to talking.

I look at Garth.

We smile at each other but don't say anything.

Garth is one of the quietest people I've ever met.

He is cute, very cute.

For some reason, that makes me nervous, very nervous.

The most he's talked to me was when he told me that we were both on the paper.

Mrs. Lipschitz comes over to us and starts talking about what a great job we've done.

There's something that I want to ask but I'm a little afraid to ask.

I say it anyway: "I know I'm one of the artists, but do you think I could write an article, too . . . freelance . . . my family and I are going to Plymouth, Massachusetts, and I thought that maybe I could write a travel column."

She thinks about it. "I don't think we've ever had a travel column before. It might be fun to try out. Talk to Eric about it."

Garth says, "Plymouth . . . that's the Pilgrims, right? Next month is Thanksgiving. That would be a good time for an article about that."

I look at Garth.

I like him more and more every time he opens his mouth.

If he actually talked more, I'd probably be totally in like with him right now.

I'm going to try to talk with him more, too.

He's not the only shy person.

I'm a little shy, too, especially with people I don't know or don't know well.

I look at Mrs. Lipschitz. "And we're going to visit lots of other places. I can report on those, too."

She smiles and nods. Then she goes over to talk with Louie.

I stand still for a while, having a little argument with myself. . . . Should I go over and ask Eric . . . I shouldn't go . . . he'd only say no . . . but I want to write the column.

I just hope that he doesn't take out his anger at Heather on all girls, especially all sixth-grade girls.

I think about the column.

GUM wanted people to know how wonderful travel is.

Writing a column will let me show that.

Taking a deep breath, I walk over to Eric.

"Eric," I say.

"Yeah." He has icing on his nose.

It's hard to be nervous with someone who has icing on his nose.

I tell him about my idea for a travel column.

"Great," he says. "It's your assignment. Include a picture with the article."

I nod and then walk back to my desk.

I am going to be doing a travel column. That's so exciting.
It'll be all about Skate Tate and Family on the road. . . .
I'll call the column "United Tates of America."
Now I'm really getting excited about going to Plymouth.
In fact, I can't wait.

Chapter 18

Are we there yet?" Emma says for the eighty gazillionth time.

Sometimes my sister drives me nuts because she can be an annoying pain, an immature squirmy person, one who is so easily bored that she can't even amuse herself.

This is one of those times.

My mother says for the eighty gazillionth time, "Emma dear. Can't you find SOMETHING to amuse yourself?"

Emma says, "No," for the eighty gazillionth time.

I look up from my book. "I can tell you, she's not amusing me, either."

Emma pouts, squirms, squirms and pouts. "I am so bored . . . and I have to go to the bathroom."

My father says, "As soon as we see a rest area, we'll stop."

"Rest area," I say. "Why don't they call it what it is. A pee area."

Actually we've been on the road for a long time, and I'm getting a little squirmy too. "Pee area . . . Pee area . . . isn't that a city in Illinois?"

My father laughs.

My mother sighs.

"It's the capital of Illinois," Emma says.

"Springfield," I say. "That's the capital of Illinois. Peoria is just a city in Illinois."

GUM would be proud of me for remembering that.

"Whatever." Emma sighs. "Are we at the rest area yet? I really have to REST."

I laugh and then say, "If you didn't drink so much soda on the way up, you wouldn't have to REST so much."

My dad says, "The sign says one mile to the next area. Just hold it."

We take the right and go up the road to the restaurant–rest area.

Emma rushes in.

My mother follows her.

My dad and I stand by the van and stretch.

I pat our brand-new van, our first not-used vehicle. "Good job, Vincent."

Dad and Mom bought it last week for our trips.

Dad says, "GUM would have approved. He'd be glad that we bought a vehicle that will travel so well, and he would have loved the name you gave it."

I was so proud when I thought of its name, Vincent VAN Go.

While we wait for Mom and Emma, Dad and I clean out the car.

There are many food wrappers in it . . . empty water bottles . . . empty soda cans . . . used Kleenexes. (Emma has a little cold . . . and she's practicing her crying some more.)

Dad picks up the book I'm reading. "*Maus*. Great book . . . not easy going, though."

I nod. "Not easy. I borrowed it from my friend Garth, who said that it is an important book for us as readers and as artists."

I think about the book, how it's a comic strip about the Holocaust . . . well, actually not a comic strip . . . Garth says that it's called a "graphic novel."

My dad says, "That's very grown up. I'm pleased to see you reading so much."

I am so happy that my dad is very pleased with me.

He picks up my sketchbook.

It's opened to a picture of Emma that I've been working on.

"Skate, this is really good." He looks at me. "You really are serious about becoming an artist, aren't you?"

I nod.

He smiles. "That's great. I knew when I was your age that I wanted to be a teacher. Other kids wanted to be actors, or rock stars or sport stars. I wanted to be a history teacher."

"You're doing exactly what you planned to do in sixth grade?"
I never realized that about my dad.

He nods. "Mostly . . . I thought I would be teaching in a high school . . . but I love teaching at the college."

I'm glad that he's teaching at the college, too.

Even though I love him, I don't think I would want him to be my teacher in school.

That would be too weird.

I like the fact that my dad takes me seriously.

I like the fact that I'm having this time alone with my dad, just to talk.

When the family goes on vacation, there's not much time alone with anyone . . . except for Emma, because when we travel, she and I share the room that is next to my parents. Sometimes that's fun and sometimes it's not.

My dad looks at me. "Skate. I have a question."

"Yes?"

He grins. "Your new friend Garth?"

I don't know what he's going to say.

Sometimes my dad gets weird about guys.

He's been teasing me about them since I was in preschool and came home and told them that Benny Seagram asked me to marry him.

Dad was relieved that I said no.

I said no because Benny was not a LEGOs sharer and because he said that I would have to bring him peanut butter and banana sandwiches and because I was only four.

"Dad," I say. "He's an artist. He doesn't say much. It's not a romance. I'm only eleven."

"Just checking." He grins.

Sometimes I can't tell when my dad is teasing and when he's not.

Mom and Emma return.

We get back in the car.

Emma is much happier now.

We start singing "We're off to see the Pilgrims" to the tune of "We're off to see the wizard."

When Emma and I are done with the song, my dad says, "Now don't forget . . . the Pilgrims weren't the only people who came over on the *Mayflower*. Among the 102 people who arrived, some left England for religious reasons and some for economic ones."

Having a father who is a history teacher means that we hear a lot of history, even when we're not in school.

He continues, "They referred to themselves as the Saints and the Strangers."

I think about the people who went to Plymouth in 1620.

I think about the people who are going there now . . . us . . . the Tates.

I think about how the word "us" uses the same letters as U.S., the United States.

We're not saints.

We're a little strange, but I hope that we're not strangers.

Vincent VAN Go is not the *Mayflower* . . . but Plymouth Rock . . . we're on our way.

Chapter 19

I don't believe it.

There's a duck-crossing sign in Plymouth.

And there are ducks on the lawn.

I wonder if they know that they have their own duck-crossing sign and only cross the road there.

I wonder if when the ducks get muddy, they go back and forth across the street so that people call them dirty double crossers.

. . . A duck-crossing sign . . .

Huey, Duey, and Louie would love it.

I can just imagine them in front of the sign, quacking their duck song, waddling their duck dance.

"Look at the sign," I say to my family.

My dad points to the sign. "Take a gander at that."

"What a silly goose you are." My mom grins at him.

He takes her hand and holds it as they walk across the lawn, heading to Plymouth Rock. "I'm not going to let that ruffle my feathers."

I look at my parents, who are giving each other a kiss . . . in public.

"Gross," Emma says, under her breath.

Emma gets very embarrassed when our parents kiss in public.

I only get a little bit embarrassed when they do that, as long as it isn't one of those long kisses that people on television do a lot.

I put Mr. Smiley Face next to Emma's face and have him give her a kiss.

Looking around to make sure that no one is looking, she giggles again.

"So are you going to ask someone to hold Mr. Smiley Face in front of Plymouth Rock?" she asks.

I shrug. "Don't know . . . I'm going to have to think about it. It makes me a little nervous. I don't want strangers to think I'm weird."

Emma giggles again. "Your friends and family all think that you're weird. Why shouldn't strangers?"

I hit her over the head with Mr. Smiley Face.

We get to the Plymouth Rock monument.

The outside looks like the pictures of Greek temples. It has twelve columns.

When we went to Plimoth Plantation yesterday, the buildings looked like the original settlement was supposed to.

I don't understand why an American symbol is in something that looks like a Greek temple. Personally, I think it should look like something that people would have built in colonial times.

We walk in, lean on a railing, and look down.

There it is. Plymouth Rock. "1620" is chiseled on it.

"It's a rock," Emma says.

"Duh," I say. "Of course Plymouth Rock is a rock . . . what did you expect it to be, a muffin? Then it would have been called Plymouth Muffin, not Plymouth Rock. It's not very big, though. I thought it would be gigantic and it looks so tiny, especially from up here."

My dad, the history teacher, does his thing. "It was once bigger, about fifteen feet long and three feet wide. Now it's about one-third of that size. And a lot of it is buried in sand. And the rock has been moved several times."

"Moved?" I look at him, surprised.

"In the beginning, no one made a big deal out of it. Then in 1741

107

someone said that the First Comers stepped on the rock when they arrived in 1620 and it became important."

"The First Comers?" I ask.

He nods. "That's what the settlers were originally called, before they were called Pilgrims."

Another family is looking at the rock, too, and listening to my dad.

The little girl throws a coin on the rock.

There are already coins on it.

My dad says, "You're supposed to get your wish if the coin lands on the rock. The money goes to the Massachusetts State Department of Conservation Fund, to fund things for the Pilgrim Memorial State Park."

I look down at where the money has been thrown.

There's a way for someone to unlock the gate below, get in, and collect the money.

They can also clean up the beer cans that some goofball has thrown in.

"How did the rock get here?" Emma asks.

We're never going to get to lunch if she asks him questions.

"Well . . . ," my dad starts, "in 1741, a ninety-five-year-old man, Thomas Faunce, said that this was the rock where the First Comers landed. He said that he had heard it from his father, who had heard it in 1623 from someone who came over on the *Mayflower*. Not everyone agreed, but over time it became an accepted fact. People wanted to have a symbol, traditions."

"Do you think it was true?" Emma asks.

My father shrugs and then continues. "I don't know. I wasn't there. I know that you think I'm old, but not that old!"

"Almost." Emma grins at him.

My father grins back. "Nothing special was done at that time. A wharf was built around the rock, and just the top part showed. Then, in 1769, people wanted to celebrate the first landing and decided to give the rock more importance."

We're only up to 1769 and my father still has a lot of facts.

This is what always happens on trips.

Our dad, Mr. History Teacher, tells us more then we ever wanted to know.

The other family leaves.

I bet they are going to get some lunch.

I never got up enough nerve to ask if they would pose with Mr. Smiley Face.

"In 1774, people first tried to move the rock. It broke and the bottom was left where it was and the top half was hauled to the Town Square, in front of the Liberty Pole. That piece broke in two but was put back together during another move in 1834."

"Yikes," I say.

He nods. "Then, in 1880, the rock was moved back to the waterfront and the two pieces from the first break were brought back together. Then, in 1920, the rock was moved again. At different times, the rock was chipped to make it fit in places. Also, people took pieces away with them and other pieces were given as gifts. There's even a piece in the Smithsonian Institute in Washington, D.C."

"Is that what they mean by a rock tour?" I strum an imaginary guitar.

We look at the rock for a while. Then we look out at the water and then up at the hill.

We people-watch. My family likes doing that. It's fun to see how people react to something, especially the rock.

Lots of people come into the portico, but I am very shy about asking them to take a picture with Mr. Smiley Face.

Some of the people videotape the rock for a few minutes.

The people are from all over the country. They are here from all over the world, speaking lots of different languages. Spanish. French. Japanese. Italian. Other languages I can't even figure out.

I think back to 1620 and the settlers' arrival.

I bet that none of those settlers could have even guessed how many people from all over the world would eventually visit.

Finally someone comes up, wearing all sorts of buttons on his vest.

He looks nice.

So does his wife.

I look over at my mom, who nods.

Taking a deep breath, I go over to him. "Sir. Would you mind if I took your picture with Mr. Smiley Face? His face will go in front of yours. Please. Oh, please."

He looks at me, then at the pillow, and then back at me.

He smiles and then he looks at his wife, who laughs. "Do it. I'll take a picture, too, so that I can scrapbook it."

"Scrapbook," Emma and I yell at the same time, jumping up and down. "We scrapbook, too."

For a minute, the lady, Emma, and I talk about the different things that we are going to put in our scrapbooks about Plymouth.

Then it's "photo-op" time.

After the picture taking, my parents and the couple, Mr. and Mrs. Ponti, start talking and then we all go out for lunch.

While we are having lunch and I'm learning how to eat a lobster, Mr. and Mrs. Ponti tell us about themselves . . . how when they retired, they sold their house, bought an RV, and are traveling all over the United States. Mrs. Ponti says that after lunch, we can see their RV and look at her scrapbooks of all the places they've visited.

I think about how we might never have gotten to meet them if it weren't for Mr. Smiley Face.

Thank you, GUM, I think.

I'm having a wonderful time.

I wish you were here.

Chapter 20

kate is a slimy fish," Emma sings, jumping up and down.

We've just gotten off the *Lobster Tales* boat.

I was having a great time on it, learning lots of interesting things.

I even held a lobster, hoping that it didn't know that I ate one of its relatives yesterday.

Then "IT" happened.

The owner held up this weird-looking fish and said that it was a skate.

He said that it was a member of the ray family.

I found out that I share MY name with an extremely weird-looking creature that smells like ammonia when contaminated.

In front of everyone, Emma yelled out that Skate was also a member of the Tate family. Then she giggled and pointed to ME.

There should be a law against younger sisters ever saying anything to embarrass older sisters.

A crew member said that skates are different from other members of that family because they lack a tail barb, or stinger.

I didn't know that a creature that yucky had the same name that I do.

I could have spent my entire life not knowing that fact.

Knowing Emma, she's never going to let me forget it, and she is going to make sure that everyone in the world knows it too.

I've always liked having an unusual nickname and never minded that it was also the wheel-blade things.

I think about it.

I'm not going to let it bother me, at least not much.

I'm going to use my own barb or stinger and find something that will really embarrass Emma, so that when she starts on the "Skate is slimy" thing, I'm going to be able to say something that will stop her from mentioning it.

As we walk along the waterfront, we hear someone honk.

It's the driver on the Splashdown Amphibious Duck Boat Tour.

We took that yesterday. (Huey, Duey, and Louie would love it here.) The duck boats are from the 1940s and they are sort of combo car-boats. They drive all around town and then go to the edge of the water and drive into the water, and it's like we're in a boat. The driver tells facts about Plymouth and jokes about ducks.

We wave to the driver and we walk on.

And we walk.

And we walk.

"Mom, Dad," Emma says. "Let's shop."

My parents sigh.

They think that trips are for sight-seeing, not for shopping.

Personally, I think that a museum is only as good as the gift shop. (The Plymouth Wax Museum has a great gift shop.)

"It's T-time," Emma says, as we enter a store.

When she says that, I know a lot of people think that she is talking about teatime . . . but she's not.

"T" stands for tacky, meaning having no style, being sort of tasteless.

It's a family tradition that, once each trip, we walk around a touristy store and each of us picks out the tackiest thing. Since we don't want the store owners to feel bad, we don't use the word "tacky," we just say "T."

We separate and look around the store.

"This is very T." My dad holds up a Pilgrim couple salt and pepper shakers.

I nod and show him a stuffed toy that says, "Now this is a stuffed turkey."

My mom comes over with a tray that has written on it, "Pass the Turkey, Turkey."

Emma joins us. On her head she is carrying a pot of flowers, only instead of things with petals, there are boats on the stems . . . Mayflowers.

Emma wins.

We each buy something but not the "T" thing that we have picked out. That's just to show.

I buy the snow globe. Emma buys the license-plate key chain with her name on it. I can't get one of them because none of the name things ever have my name on it. Not only am I now a slimy fish-name person but I am an unable-to-have-my-name-on-souvenir-things person. Sometimes, life is just not perfect.

I also buy a present for Susie, a really great T-shirt.

We've always bought things for each other when we go places without each other.

I'm not sure that I would have bought it, except Susie bought a T-shirt for me when she and Kiki and the rest of that group went to a Broadway play.

I haven't worn it yet.

It's off for more sight-seeing.

"Burial Hill next," my father says. "That's where people are just dying to get in."

"Not funny." Emma stamps her foot and yells. "Don't make jokes about it."

She starts to cry.

One minute she's fine.

Next minute she's not.

She's thinking about GUM.

I know she is.

It's hard to hear someone make a joke about dying, especially our own dad.

Dad says, "Emma, please calm down now. When we get there, we'll talk about this."

"I don't want to go," Emma sobs.

I stand there quietly.

I don't want to go to the cemetery, either.

My father looks at us and then he softly says, "Okay, we won't go to Burial Hill right away. Instead, let's go sit on that bench in front of the wax museum."

We walk up the hill.

My father has his arm around Emma's shoulder.

My mother comes up and puts her arm around me.

It's time for a Tate family talk.

Chapter 21

mma cries and cries and cries.
I really haven't seen her cry since GUM's memorial service.

Dad has his arm around her, and then Mom goes over to her, too.

I just sit there on the grass watching.

I don't think anyone could have loved GUM more than I did.

Mom is stroking Emma's hair.

Dad is hugging Emma and looking over her head at Mom.

They all just sit there.

I feel a little left out but don't think it's a good idea to go over there right now.

Emma looks up.

She's crying so hard that her nose is running.

Mom takes a tissue out of her handbag and hands it to Emma, who immediately wipes her eyes and blows into the tissue.

I'm glad that Emma did it that way instead of blowing her nose first and then wiping her eyes.

Emma tries to catch her breath. "I don't think you should make jokes about people dying. What about GUM?"

"GUM used to like jokes," Dad says. "I'm sorry that one upset you, though, so I won't say it again."

"Good." Emma sniffles.

"We all miss him a lot, don't we?" Dad ruffles Emma's hair.

We all nod.

I move closer to my family, and we sit in a circle.

Emma is leaning on my mom.

My dad holds my hand.

"I miss him so much," I say.

I decide I have to make a confession. "I feel really bad. Just before he died, I wished that we had a lot more money . . . and then he died . . . and now we do. It's my fault for wishing that."

Emma starts to cry again, a lot. "It's not your fault. It's mine. I was really bad. I made him promise to come to my class. . . . I made him say, "'Cross my heart and hope to die.' . . . It's all my fault. It really is. I know it."

I cry. "Emma. Maybe it's both our faults, not just one of us."

Mom immediately says, "I want the two of you to listen to me . . . and listen to me carefully."

We look up at her.

She takes both of our hands. "Neither of you separately nor together are powerful enough to cause someone's death by what you say or feel. You are not responsible. You didn't run over him with a car. You didn't do anything violent. GUM died because he had a heart condition."

I sigh.

So does Emma.

I guess we've both been keeping this inside of us since it happened.

My dad holds our hands, too. "It's not any of our faults. Mom can tell you that I was feeling guilty, too, because I didn't try to stop him from going away after he found out about his heart condition. I tried once and he got angry at me, so I stopped trying to tell him what to do."

"No one's fault," Mom says, softly. "Not GUM's either . . . he wanted to live . . . he was taking the medicine that he was supposed to. I guess it was just his time."

117

"It was a bad time," I say. "He wasn't *that* old."

"There's never a good time to lose someone we love. Nor do people who love life as much as GUM did want to leave life. But it happens." My dad lets go of my hand and wipes tears from his eyes.

I think about how GUM was like a father to him and how his own father died so young.

"Daddy." I take his hand again. "Is your heart okay?"

I've always wanted to ask him that but was afraid to . . . afraid that he wouldn't like to think about it and afraid of the answer.

He nods. "After GUM died, I went to the doctor for a major checkup. I'm fine."

My mom says, "I think that it's a good idea to let the girls know things . . . or they will worry again . . . or not believe us."

They look at each other and then my father nods again. "Girls. I'm not lying to you. I am fine. My blood pressure is a little high. I'm taking medication for it . . . but I'm fine. The doctor said that since there is a history of heart trouble for the men in my family, I have to be very careful. I am being careful. So you shouldn't worry."

"Or when you do worry" — my mom squeezes our hands lightly — "tell us so that we can talk about it. I think that we've all been so upset by what happened with GUM. We haven't all talked about it together and I think that was a mistake. I'm sorry."

"Me too," my dad says.

"I'm sorry too," I say.

"Me too." Emma nods.

"We're a pretty sorry family, aren't we?" my dad jokes.

This time Emma isn't upset by the joking. She giggles.

"Dad." There's one more thing that I want to tell him. "I promise not to do anything that will upset you, that will cause you to have a heart attack."

"Me too." Emma starts to cross her heart (and hope to die), but stops herself.

She hits one hand with the other.

My dad looks very serious. "Girls. I want you to understand something. You cannot cause me to have a heart attack. Don't ever believe that one person can do that to another. If I have one, it's because of my family history, or because it just happens, or because I am not taking care of myself appropriately. And I plan to take care of myself. So if anything happens, it's not because you caused it or I caused it."

We all sit quietly for a minute and then Mom says, "Do you all feel better now?"

I nod.

Emma nods.

My dad nods.

Mom nods back.

She smiles. "GUM would be so glad that we've talked all of this out."

"And he'd be glad that we talked here, sitting on Coles Hill," my dad tells us.

"Why on Coles Hill?" my mom asks.

Emma and I look at each other.

Something tells me that the history teacher part of my dad is going to make a return.

He explains. "Coles Hill is the place that the settlers hid the bodies of those who died in the first year, in unmarked graves. They did that so that the Native Americans didn't know how small the group had become."

"Are the bodies buried under us?" I make a face.

"No." He points at something. "As the bones of the settlers were found in later years, they were collected and many of them are in the sarcophagus."

"Who is the statue of?" Emma asks.

"Massasoit. He was the chief of the Wampanoags. They befriended the settlers and taught them survival skills."

The ground that we are sitting on is like a history lesson coming to life.

"Look out there." My father points straight ahead. "What do you see?"

Emma and I start listing the things that we see . . . Plymouth Rock . . . the *Mayflower II* . . . the bay . . . tourists . . . people who live in Plymouth . . . boats . . . cars . . . the ducks . . .

My father asks again, "Why do you think that I say that GUM would be glad that we are having this talk here?"

This is my father, the history teacher who lets students (and his children) learn for themselves.

I answer. "The settlers had to be brave and take chances and learn new things and —"

Emma cuts in. "And meet new people . . . and make new friends . . . and learn to live together."

I continue. "And even when they were afraid, go ahead."

Dad nods. "Yes. Trust in themselves . . . not expect to be perfect."

My mom adds, "Learn that people live and die and that life goes on."

I look out and see the tiny *Mayflower II* and think about how all those people came over and all that they did.

I think about the Indians who were already here and what they had to go through.

I see all of the people who are learning about Plymouth and think about how many people there are in the world and how many places there are in the world to learn about.

I think I am really beginning to understand GUM.

He was always a part of my life, but now I'm beginning to feel that he is a part of me, who I am, who I am becoming. I've never thought of it like this before. I think that this is the most grown-up thought I've ever had.

I always loved him, but now I feel like I'm really getting to know him and am so sorry that we won't be able to get to know each other better.

I think he would really like it that I'm beginning to understand him better.

Chapter 22

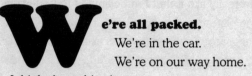

e're all packed.
We're in the car.
We're on our way home.

I think about this trip.

I think about how we visited a great place, one that GUM also saw.

I wonder if sometimes my feet stepped in exactly the same places that his did.

I think about how I'm going to be able to visit places GUM visited and also go to places that he never got to see.

Emma looks at me and says, "So, Skate the fish, how does it feel to be leaving a place with a waterfront?"

Ignoring her for now, I put it on a list in my brain that I will have to torment her a little when I have time.

Picking up my knapsack, I take out my wallet, open it, and pull out the money from India that GUM gave out the day he visited my class.

Sometimes I wonder how I can feel so sad one moment and so good another . . . and even feel a mixture of the two at other times.

I remember the day he came to class, and I smile.

He really did drive the principal over the edge and he never had to use the steering wheel to do it.

Then I think about his memorial service.

Sad thoughts . . . happy thoughts . . . sad thoughts.

I give the rupees a little kiss because it was once GUM's and put it back in my wallet.

I think about all of the places we've seen, the things that we've done, and the people we've met.

I think about how I have to write everything in my journal so that I can remember to include things in my scrapbook. I also start thinking about the Plymouth Game that I am going to make up. I'm going to put the pages in my scrapbook. Dad, who asked that I do the game, is going to show it to his class as the model for an assignment that he is going to give them. Pressure. It's a lot of pressure to make sure that I do this well.

My dad is driving and singing "On the Road Again."

My mom is smiling and covering her ears because of my dad's voice.

Emma has already opened our trip snack pack and is trying to hide the fact that she is eating ALL of the cookies.

She's getting crumbs all over Mr. Smiley Face.

I think about what GUM said when he gave me Mr. Smiley Face.

He said that if I took Mr. Smiley Face with me wherever I went, even if GUM couldn't be with me, it would be like he's there.

Well, he was right.

I do feel that way.

I also feel that even if Mr. Smiley Face is not with me, GUM is with me in so many ways.

I also remember what GUM told me once, that I shouldn't be afraid of what's "around the corner," that I should be excited thinking about it and if something is not good, just deal with it. He said that I should be at least interested and hopefully excited to find out what is there.

Around the corner, here I come.

Susie

The Happy Scrappys

Skate

SKATE

TO DO:
1. Think of new I.A. project: Scrapbook Organizer????
2. Call friends.
3. Practice handwriting and printing (for scrapbooking).
4. Try to get organized.
5. Remind Emma not to borrow my clothes.
6. Brush Tunaburger's teeth- Aaaaaaaarg!!!!!!!!!!
7. Work on cartoon.
8. Call Garth-Maybe! Maybe Not!

DAISY DAYS

HAPPY Birthday

♥ BOOKS

♥ BASEBALL

♥ BIRTHDAYS

SCHOOL PICTURES

K
They did NOT let me bring my "Blankie" to school. I cried!

1
When the photographer said, "Say Cheese", I went "Grrrrrrrrrr" instead.

2
Grandma asked me to wear this dress-- aaaaaaaaaarg!!!!!

3
"YOU SNOT BALL!" I am saying to Joey Braun.

I got detention!!!!!

THE D.D.T. - Doing the duck dance

huey duey louie

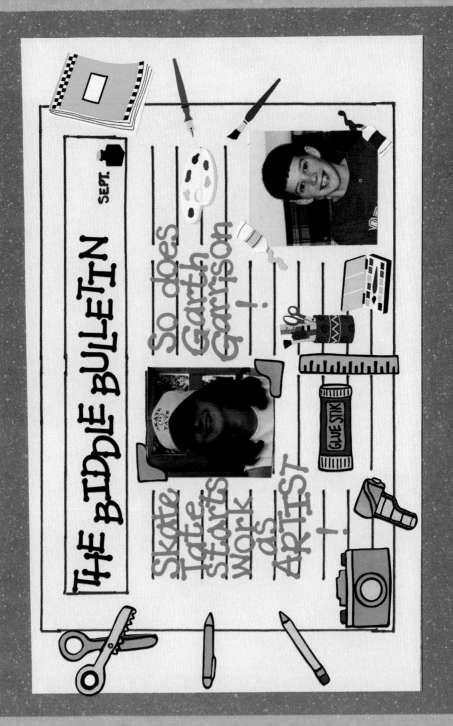

VERY PUNNY

BORED

SKATE—

SKATE—

BOARD

Lunch Time

PLYMOUTH ROCK
LANDING PLACE OF THE
PILGRIMS
1620

at the duck boat tour

MR. SMILEY GOES

TO **PLYMOUTH·MASS.**

at Plimoth Plantation

WELCOME
to the
17th century.

Mr. Ponti

Funny Plymouth Sights

LIVE BAIT & SODA - I made sure that I pushed the right button!

duck crossing

EMMA TAKES PHOTOS OF REAR ENDS - real & statue

WE TOOK NO HERRING!

TAKING HERRING PROHIBITED

PLYMOUTH
NATIONAL WAX MUSEUM

FACTS ABOUT THE PLYMOUTH NATIONAL WAX MUSEUM

1. The figures are not wax! The place should be called The Plymouth National Wax-like Compound Museum.

2. There are 25 scenes about the journey to Plymouth.

3. Emma bought a rock in the gift shop. It had "Plymouth Rock" written on it. It probably came from N.J.

This place is so much fun. Mr. Smiley LOVED it!

plymouth:signs

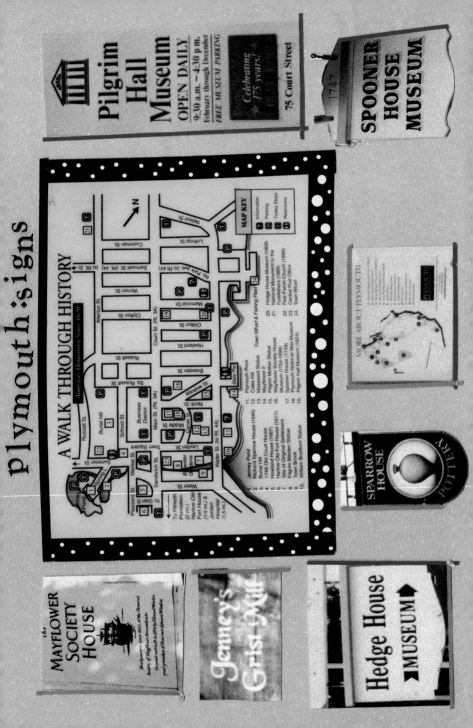

Pilgrim Hall Museum

OPEN DAILY
9:30 a.m. — 4:30 p.m.
February through December

FREE MUSEUM PARKING

Celebrating 175 years

75 Court Street

1747

SPOONER HOUSE MUSEUM

A WALK THROUGH HISTORY

America's Hometown Since 1620

N

MAP KEY

- P Information
- P Parking
- T Trolley Stops
- R Restrooms

1. Jenney Pond
2. Richard Sparrow House (1640)
3. Burial Hill
4. 1749 Court House
5. Howland House (1667)
6. Harlow Old Fort House (1677)
7. Site of Original Settlement
8. Pilgrim Maiden Statue
9. Town Brook
10. William Bradford Statue
11. Plymouth Rock
12. Coles Hill
13. Massasoit Statue
14. Mayflower II
15. Pilgrim Mother Statue
16. Mayflower Society House
17. Sparrow House (1749)
18. Plymouth National Wax Museum
19. Pilgrim Hall Museum (1824)
20. Hedge House Museum (1809)
21. Pilgrims Monument to the Forefathers
22. First Parish Church (1899)
23. Central Post Office
24. Town Wharf

Town Wharf & Fishing Fleet

To Plymouth
Plantation
(2 mi.)
Harlow Old
Fort House
(1/4 mi.) &
Jordan
Hospital
(1.5 mi.)

MORE ABOUT PLYMOUTH

SPARROW HOUSE

POTTERY

---

the
MAYFLOWER SOCIETY HOUSE

Jenney's Grist-Mill

Hedge House
◄ MUSEUM

PLIMOTH PLANTATION

The Pilgrim Village, Hobbamock's Homesite, the Crafts Center and the Mayflower II...we stepped into the 17th Century...and yes, they spell it Plimoth.

On the original Mayflower, there were 102 passengers and 30 crew....BUT there were NO bathrooms....AND they sailed for 66 days and nights. (I wonder what the poop deck was used for?!?!?!)And there were NO hairdryers! I'm glad I live in the 21st Century!

PILGRIMS!

IF APRIL SHOWERS BRING MAY FLOWERS, WHAT DO MAY FLOWERS BRING?

I was so excited to find a lobster punch. I glued them on and then my Dad said that they are Scorpions, not Lobsters!!!!! Oh well....No "Claws" for concern!!!!!!

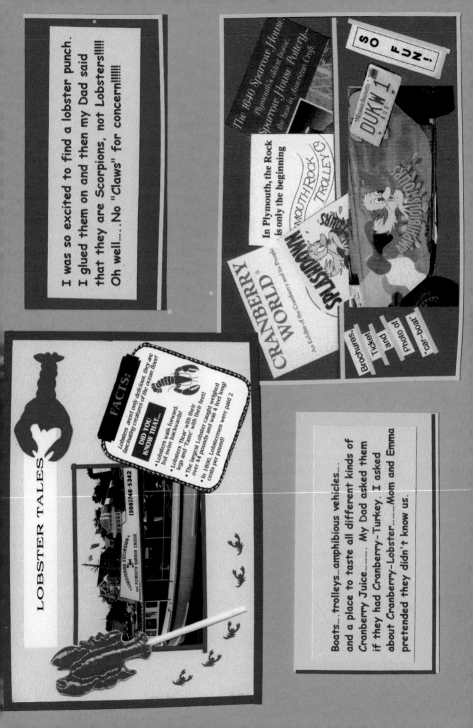

The 1640 Sparrow House...
Sparrow House Pottery...
Plymouth's oldest home
the best in American Craft.

In Plymouth, the Rock is only the beginning

MONTHROCK TROLLEY ©

CRANBERRY WORLD ®
An Exhibit of the Cranberry and Its People

SPLASHDOWN

AMPHIBIOUS TOURS

Massachusetts
DUKW 1 BUS

S O N U T !

Brochures,
Ticket
and
Photo of
"car-boat"

LOBSTER TALES

FACTS:
Lobsters aren't only delicious, they are fascinating creatures of the ocean floor!

DID YOU KNOW THAT...
• Lobsters walk forward, but swim backwards!
• Lobsters 'Hear' with their legs and 'Taste' with their feet!
• The largest Lobster caught weighed over 44 pounds and was 4 feet long!
• In 1880 Lobstermen were paid 2 cents per pound!

(508)746-5342
LOBSTERING EXCURSION
and PLYMOUTH HARBOR CRUISE

Boats...trolleys...amphibious vehicles... and a place to taste all different kinds of Cranberry Juice........ My Dad asked them if they had Cranberry-Turkey. I asked about Cranberry-Lobster.......Mom and Emma pretended they didn't know us.

leega   Burial Hill, Plymouth, Mass

Visiting Burial Hill reminded me that people have always lived and died.
When I was walking around and looking at the tombstones, I thought
about GUM......how even though he is dead, he will always be alive in
my heart.

Massachusetts Symbols

THE BAY STATE

Seal

SIGILLUM REIPUBLICÆ MASSACHUSETTENSIS

FLAG

The 6th State

STATE EMBLEMS:
muffin-corn
cookie-chocolate chip
dessert-boston cream pie
berry-cranberry
beverage-cranberry juice
fossil-dinosaur tracks
bean-navy bean
heroine-Deborah Samson
hero-Johnny Appleseed

capital-Boston

Mayflower

bird

chickadee

dog

boston terrier

horse

morgan

folk dance

square dancing

fish

cod

insect

ladybug

PLYMOUTH ROCK & ROLL*

GAME PIECES

1620 1620 1620 1620 1620

START

TAKE KNOWLEDGE CARD

MOVE TO NEXT

OBJECT OF GAME - WIN

Rules:
#1. Roll die and move, and rock.
#2. Don't cheat! your move if you win.
#3. Don't whine if you lose.
#4. Don't gloat if you win.
#5. Enjoy your Tour of MASS.

KNOWLEDGE CARDS:

WHAT BOY'S ALMOST BLEW UP THE SHIP?

WHO WAS BORN ON THE SHIP?

WHO WAS SQUANTO?

WAS THE MAYFLOWER COMPACT SOMETHING TO DO WITH MAKE-UP?

HOW LONG DID THE VOYAGE LAST?

HOW FAR IS PLYMOUTH FROM BOSTON?

WHERE IS THE PUBLIC LIBRARY?

NAME FOUR PEOPLE WHO CAME OVER ON THE MAYFLOWER.

ON THE MAYFLOWER, WHERE WAS THE POOP DECK?

Answer Correctly: Move 3 spaces

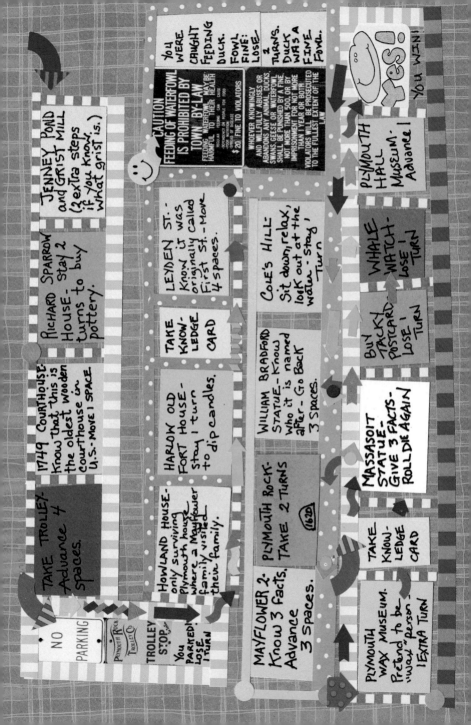

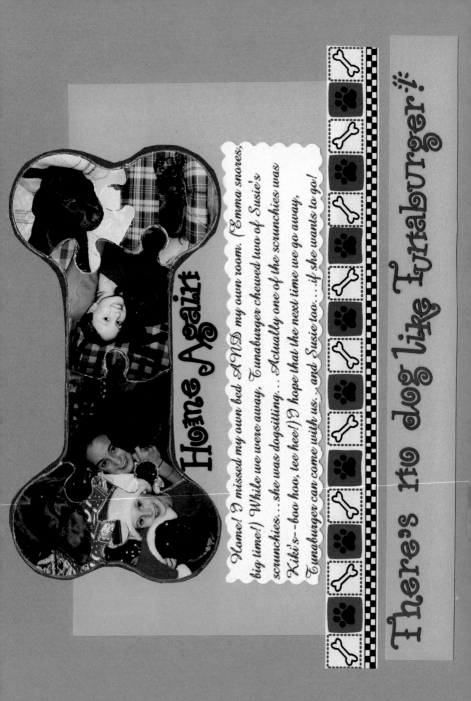

Home Again

Home! I missed my own bed AND my own room. (Emma snores, big time!) While we were away, Tunaburger chewed two of Susie's scrunchies... she was dogsitting... Actually one of the scrunchies was Kiki's-- boo hoo, tee hee!) I hope that the next time we go away, Tunaburger can come with us... and Susie too... if she wants to go!

There's no dog like Tunaburger!

Scrapbook Credits

page 1: Family and Friends
lettering: creative letters from Making Memories
paper (jellybean): ©Hot Off The Press, Inc.

pages 2–3: The Happy Scrappys
lettering: ©me & my BIG ideas
die-cuts: ©Ellison
stickers: S.R.M.®

page 4: Susie
lettering: creative letters from Making Memories
sticker designs by Mrs. Grossman's Paper Company
"jewels": from India

page 5: Skate
alphabet lettering: Frances Meyer, Inc.®
die-cut of clipboard: ©Ellison
"To Do" sticker designs by Mrs. Grossman's Paper Company
font: Nuptial Script

page 6: Emma
lettering: ©me & my BIG ideas
star die-cuts: ©Ellison
sticker designs by Mrs. Grossman's Paper Company

page 7: Liberty
lettering and sticker designs by Mrs. Grossman's Paper Company

page 8: Daisy
daisy name lettering: Frances Meyer, Inc.®
daisy stickers: ©me & my BIG ideas
heart sticker designs by Mrs. Grossman's Paper Company

page 9: Two Smart Cookies
lettering: creative letters from Making Memories
cooking and milk stickers: Stickopotamus® Stickers
design lines and caption sticker designs by Mrs. Grossman's Paper Company
cookies: Ashley, Alex, and Joni

pages 10–11: School Pictures
Computer font: CK Boxed, "The Best of Creative Lettering" CD-Combo, Creating Keepsakes
numbers: Making Memories
big pushpin stickers: Stickopotamus® Stickers
little pushpin sticker designs by Mrs. Grossman's Paper Company
picture sticker: ©me & my BIG ideas
scissors: Fiskars, Inc. (alligator)
font: CAC Krazy Legs Bold

page 12: Donald Duck Trio
background paper: Keeping Memories Alive, Inc.
duck paper: Pixie Press
lettering (boys' names): creative letters from Making Memories
lettering (The D.D.T., etc.): Provo Craft®
design lines by Mrs. Grossman's Paper Company
duck stickers: Provo Craft®

page 13: The Biddle Bulletin
art sticker designs (for Garth) by Mrs. Grossman's Paper Company
scrapbooking stickers (for Skate): Frances Meyer, Inc.®
paper: Keeping Memories Alive, Inc.
newspaper template: "Read All About It" by Chatterbox, the Journaling Genie

page 14: GUM's Birthday
paper: The Paper Patch®
lettering: Frances Meyer, Inc.®
heart sticker (used as an apostrophe) design by Mrs. Grossman's Paper Company

page 15: Gone Fishing
lettering: creative letters from Making Memories
page topper: Cock-A-Doodle Design, Inc.
design lines and arrow sticker designs by Mrs. Grossman's Paper Company
fishing paper: The Paper Patch®
smiley sticker: TREND enterprises, Inc.
font: Comic Sans Ms.

page 16: Very Punny
lettering: creative letters from Making Memories
design lines and skateboard sticker designs by Mrs. Grossman's Paper Company

page 17: Our Trip
lettering: creative letters from Making Memories
die-cut signposts: ©Ellison
van: Paula Danziger drawing
sign paper: ©Hot Off The Press, Inc.

pages 18–19: Mr. Smiley Goes to Plymouth
lettering: creative letters from Making Memories
computer font: "Doodle Crayon," PagePrintables volume 1 CD, Cock-A-Doodle Design, Inc.
design lines and heart sticker designs by Mrs. Grossman's Paper Company

page 20: Funny Plymouth Sights
lettering: creative letters from Making Memories
paper (background): from India
card stock: Keeping Memories Alive, Inc.

page 21: Plymouth Wax Museum
computer font: "Dipsy Doodle," PagePrintables volume 1 CD, Cock-A-Doodle Design, Inc.
design lines and numbers by Mrs. Grossman's Paper Company

page 22: Plymouth Signs
design lines by Mrs. Grossman's Paper Company

page 23: Plymouth Rock
lettering and box stickers: S.R.M.®
caption sticker designs by Mrs. Grossman's Paper Company

page 24: Plimoth Plantation
paper: The Paper Patch®
design lines by Mrs. Grossman's Paper Company
scissors: Fiskars, Inc. (scallop)
font: Goudy Handtooled D
permissions: Plimoth Plantation is a trademark of Plimoth Plantation. Photographs taken with permission from Plimoth Plantation.
alphabet block stickers: Frances Meyer, Inc.®

page 25: Mayflower II
paper: The Paper Patch®
stickers: ©me & my BIG ideas
scissors: Fiskars, Inc. (seagull)
caption sticker designs by Mrs. Grossman's Paper Company
font: Mariage D
permissions: Mayflower II is a trademark of Plimoth Plantation. Photographs taken with permission from Plimoth Plantation.

page 26: Lobster Tales, Splashdown Amphibious Tours, and brochures
lobster die-cut: Accu-Cut Systems
design lines by Mrs. Grossman's Paper Company
scorpion punch: Nankong
permissions: Lobster Tales, Inc., and Splashdown Amphibious Tours™

page 27: Burial Hill
photo credit: Helga Stottmeier
font: BibleScrT

pages 28–29: Massachusetts Symbols
lettering: creative letters from Making Memories
die-cut of Massachusetts: ©Ellison
emblems (except for square dancing): Gallopade International, Inc.
square-dancing emblem: Paula Danziger, using stickers by Mrs. Grossman's Paper Company
design lines by Mrs. Grossman's Paper Company
paper: Keeping Memories Alive, Inc.
font: Tahoma

pages 30–31: Plymouth Rock and Roll
lettering: creative letters by Making Memories
Mayflower die-cut: ©Ellison
arrow sticker designs by Mrs. Grossman's Paper Company
smiley face stickers: TREND enterprises, Inc.

page 32: Home Again
lettering: creative letters from Making Memories
dog bone and paw border: S.R.M.®
scissors: Fiskars, Inc. (scallop)
dog bone: Coluzzle™ Cutting System by Provo Craft
font: Amazone BT

Special Acknowledgments

To Jeanne Maloney — who deserves so much credit for helping to get permissions to use products, for helping to keep me organized and on task, and for being a wonderful friend.

To the Grays — Joni, Skip, Ashley, McKenzie, and Taylor, also wonderful friends. Without them the scrapbook portion of this book would have been very different . . . I am so very grateful to all of them, especially Joni who took so many of the pictures, organized "models," and who is my "scrapbooking pal" . . . and such a good friend!

To the other terrific people in the scrapbook — Alexandra Arnold, Chanté Jones, Nate Sexton, Danjai Jones, Michael Carroll, Ryan Carroll, Cameron Hoellrich, Jim and Jean Middaugh, the Raab guys — David, Brian, Jeffrey, and Joshua — Carrie Danziger, Ben Danziger, and Matthew Hardin.

To the Group in Plymouth: Lee Regan and everyone else at Plymouth Public Library, and Helga Stottmeier — for being such a wonderful photographer and allowing me to use her picture of Burial Hill.

To the people of Plymouth; also to the people who are in charge of the attractions that I visited in Plymouth.

To the "amateur" photographers, other than myself — Annette Danziger, Joshua Danziger, Joni Gray, Susan Raab (and to all the parents of the kids in the book who supplied permission and photos).

TO SO MANY WONDERFUL PEOPLE IN THE WORLD OF SCRAPBOOKING! There are so many individuals that to list them would take up the space of an entire novel . . . but there are some who have been especially helpful and kind and informative:

Andrea Grossman and everyone who works with her — especially Alison Hastings, Sherryl Kumli, and Sue Ferguson (who ran a special workshop just for me) . . . and Beau and Angus (the wonder dogs).

Dee Gruenig of Posh Impressions.

Everyone at Creating Keepsakes magazine, especially Lisa Bearnson, Debbie Hanni, Stacy Dill, Valerie Pingree, Merrilynne Harrington, Becky Higgins, Emily Johnson, Deanna and Don Lambson, Kim McCrary, Mark Seastrand, Tom Stuber, and Tracy White.

Sara Naumann of Hot Off The Press.

Nancy and Dale Bohrer of Dream Events, Inc. (and to everyone I met at the Scrappers Dream Vacations) and all the terrific scrapbook stores I have visited around the country (especially to B. J. and Mark Russell of B. J.'s Scrapbooks).

And to Memory Makers magazine and Creating Keepsakes magazine, two great sources of information and inspiration.

Now on to my Writing-Artist pals:

To Bruce Coville, who once again listened to my novel in progress and offered great suggestions (he is the one who thought of naming the car "Van Go" . . . I wish I had thought of it!).

To Liz Levy — as always, a wonderful "sounding board" and great friend.

To Sandra Steen and Susan Steen — friendship in stereo!

To Marc Brown — for the support of my art and his suggestions to make it better.

Now for the Scholastic "Gang" — A GREAT TEAM —

Craig Walker — whose excitement about and support of this book was so important from the beginning . . . so terrific!

Liz Szabla — who is so supportive, so incisive, so good.

Kate Egan — who is a "Shining Star" of new editorial talent.

David Saylor — the art director who said, "Of course you can do it, Paula. Your home is a scrapbook."

Steve Scott — an art director of talent and vision.

Paul Colin — who not only assisted Steve in the design of the book but who taught me to use my new computer and my new scanner . . . a Herculean task!

With Thanks

There were so many wonderful companies who offered permissions. Although I was unable to use all of the products in the book, I want to thank everyone.

So much thanks and appreciation to all of the companies: Accu-Cut Systems; Bo-Bunny Press; Canson, Inc.; Chatterbox, Inc.; Cock-A-Doodle Design, Inc.; Creating Keepsakes magazine; Creative Teaching Press, Inc.; Current, Inc.; Cut-it-Up™; Delta Technical Coatings, Inc.; Ellison; Fiskars, Inc.; Frances Meyer, Inc.; Gallopade International, Inc.; Hambly Studios; Hero Arts Rubber Stamps, Inc.; Hot Off The Press, Inc.; Keeping Memories Alive, Inc.; Magnetic Collectables; Making Memories; me & my BIG ideas; Memory Preserves; Mrs. Grossman's Paper Company; NagPosh; Nankong; NRN Designs; Paper Adventures™, The Paper Patch®; Pixie Press; Provo Craft®; Puzzle Mates™; River City Rubber Works; S.R.M.®; Scrap-Ease®; Stampendous, Inc.®; Stickopatamus® Stickers; Teacher Created Materials, Inc.; TREND enterprises, Inc.; Xyron laminating system.

Paula Danziger's ancestors did not come over on the Mayflower, nor did she. Since her arrival (birth), she has been busy growing up and holding a variety of jobs: gift wrapper, playground supervisor, junior high teacher and, oh yes, author. She has written over thirty books, including the ever-popular *The Cat Ate My Gymsuit* and the many Amber Brown books. Because of *United Tates of America*, Paula Danziger is now a part of the scrapbooking world. She can be seen taking photos, removing stickers from her clothing, and saying "Oh, this is a scrapbook moment."

Read these other books by Paula Danziger

PUBLISHED BY SCHOLASTIC

P.S. Longer Letter Later
(with Ann M. Martin)

Snail Mail No More
(with Ann M. Martin)

PUBLISHED BY PENGUIN PUTNAM

The Cat Ate My Gymsuit

The Pistachio Prescription

The Divorce Express

There's A Bat In Bunk Five

It's An Aardvark-Eat-Turtle World

Can You Sue Your Parents For Malpractice?

This Place Has No Atmosphere

Remember Me To Harold Square

Thames Doesn't Rhyme With James

The Matthew Martin books

The Amber Brown books

Something for Everyone

Step into unknown realms, or travel around the United States.
Read about times long gone, or step into the future. Laugh at
light-hearted revenge, or cry along as entire towns suffer
oppressive times. Take a break from your everyday
and explore a new place — it's reading like never before.

Available wherever you buy books, or use this order form!